ADVENTURES
In
Another Paradise

A Novel By
Timothy Brannan

Other Books By Timothy Brannan

Into the Elephant Grass: A Vietnam Fable

TEACH [Also Kindle Edition]

'74: A Basketball Story [Also Kindle Edition]

Manhattan Spiritual [Also Kindle Edition]

TABLE OF CONTENTS

CHAPTER 1

AMERICANS IN PARADISE

Air and water exploded. Alfred Crist's eyes followed the path of the spear drilling through the clear Caribbean water toward a seven-foot nurse shark. The shark seemed to hang in the water about thirty feet away. It was a long, difficult shot--the first ever made with the new style spear gun invented by his first mate Frenchie Bryan. As he peered through the spear churned water, he saw Frenchie's emergency signal appear . . . a red warning buoy bobbing like a float on a fisherman's line at the water's surface sixty-five feet above him. For the first time, he chuckled in his head, I think I understand a little about what it's like to be a fish.

Water sizzled just a few feet to his right. Something bumped his back and left side. When he swirled around, he found another nurse shark staring him in the face through his vortex of bubbles, its jaws agape and Teddy Morhead's spear sticking out of its head just behind its bugged-out eyes. Behind it, Teddy seemed to stand in the water brandishing his spear gun, his own version of Frenchie's experiment.

Al reflected, once again, that you couldn't be too careful when spear fishing for shark. They often ran in pairs. Even though the islanders joked about Thomian sharks being too lazy to strike, Al still wasn't convinced of that . . . not at all. He'd speared shark many times, but he never saw one that his solar plexus didn't tighten up and begin to work on his chi in a negative way. After all, under water was Mr. Shark's domain. He ruled here; not humans. No matter the size of the shark or the sophistication of the human's equipment or weapons.

Both his and Teddy's spear guns had been designed as part of a special request from the Department of the Interior, the federal bureaucracy saddled with the responsibility for all territories. The Virgin Islands was a territory paid for and owned by the United States of America much in the same way one might choose to buy a piece of seaside property to build a resort home. The spears were of a special long-range design that Frenchie had talked them into trying today, since they were going to be hiding out at sea anyway. The power of the gun when it released the spear was four to six times greater than that of a normal spear gun. Most importantly, the spear was unencumbered by any line, so its flight could be truer and considerably longer.

After Al swallowed his stomach again and mentally re-fixed his chi, he shot Teddy a thumbs up and pointed to the red buoy at the surface. Teddy returned his thumbs up sign. They began to surface gradually, keeping in mind always how deep they had been working. Al kept a close eye on Teddy, not because Teddy needed watching. He was an expert diver and spear fisherman in his own right. He didn't, however, get out of his office very much due to his line of work, so it made Al feel better to sort of watch out for him just a little without him realizing it.

The new spear guns were testing out great under some pretty heavy pressure, but he still wasn't sure how well either he or Teddy was doing after such a deep, long dive. After all, nitrogen narcosis can do strange things to you, and it does become a real prospect anywhere below sixty feet or so in the ocean. The less used to diving at those depths you are, especially for long periods of time like this, the more likely you are to succumb to the hallucinatory wiles of the sweet bitch.

Sometimes, he thought, he could be considered in a perpetual state of nitrogen narcosis, because it just didn't seem possible that almost three years had passed since Doc Streeter offered him this very special and very plush assignment working out of St. Thomas, United States Virgin Islands . . . the American Paradise.

"Let's see here. Alfred NMN Crist. Vietnam Veteran. Under orders protected by National Security Laws, awarded Bronze Star with V device and Oak Leaf Cluster, Silver Star." Doc Streeter read from a stapled copy of Al's Military 201 File with "TOP SECRET, Need To Know Eyes Only" stamped on the first page. On an original, the stamp would have been in red. That information was contained inside a folder with the original black stamp CIA Collateral Personnel File. "And, the Congressional Medal of Honor, for Christ sake, for 'actions above and beyond the call of duty during Battle of Monkey Mountain, 17 November 1968.' " They had faced each other across a severely polished myrtle conference table Doc usually reserved for private meetings. "Operations file sealed by Federal Agency Order 17 November 1968."

Doc dropped the file back into the folder and the folder onto the gleaming conference table. "Damn, lad. And, then you appeared out of nowhere. Out of nowhere on old Doc Streeter's doorstep . . . better known in those days as the United Press International Washington Bureau. "What was it?" He glanced into the folder for a few moments. Papers rattled. "Special Counter-Cultural Revolution Specialist. Yes. That's what the Front Office called you, wasn't it? Special Counter-Cultural Revolution Specialist. That was how you were introduced to me. I remember, even then, being surprised at how sanitized your files were. And, this CIA folder isn't a whole lot better even now. Don't need notes for the rest. In less than two years with the bureau, I believe you were awarded one of Pulitzer's finest for your Kent State series."

Doc always seemed amused. That day four years ago he seemed even more amused than usual. "Let's see, lad. Next, we went to *Time*, and you went to Singapore. There, you were a guerilla expert. Next, Bangkok and another Pulitzer for your cover feature 'The Domino That Didn't Fall' under the guise of an Asian Political Analyst.

"*Newsweek* has been our latest stopover. Your present assignment: Revolution Specialist in Central America. You've done it all, and you've done it well, lad. A sublimely executed cover for all these years."

At that point, Doc's smirk had turned into a laugh. "Yes, I knew about you from the beginning, lad. That's part of how you got that first job with me. I've known who you were since day one, but it didn't matter to me, lad. I sensed that you had great journalism in you, no matter what. And, you did, lad. You proved old Doc right more times than not, that's for sure."

Going over familiar ground. That was Doc's way of getting things said. Al wondered how many times he'd have to listen to Doc telling him how he'd known about him from the beginning like he was some kind of quota from EEO. But, Doc was a real Aristotelian. A Ben Franklin bespectacled Aristotelian. He had talked Doc into buying those glasses back in sixty-nine. Told him he'd look like John Lennon. After Lennon's assassination, there was no taking them off.

"But do you have any idea how tough it's been to get you the good assignments you deserved? Even with your recognized talent, eccentrics don't usually get on too well at this level."

"Well, you made it somehow, Doc," he remembered retaliating.

"Yeah, I guess I did at that, lad." Doc's Adam's Apple bobbed up and down amongst the drooping skin of his neck like a turkey. "Maybe, now, it's your turn, lad. Maybe, now, it's your turn."

"My turn? What are you talking about, Doc? Am I not hacking it in the field any more? Or what?"

"Hacking it? Christ, Crist!" Doc had seemed a little irritated. "You're certainly hacking it. Rumor has it that you may be in line for yet another of Mr. Pulitzer's best for that death squad series." It had been the first work he had done with no hidden agenda in years . . . just straight gut journalism.

"So, that brings me to why I pulled you out of your insurrection *du jour*. I've got a proposal for you to consider, lad. A proposal that couldn't wait for your next R and R." Doc harrumphed. His turkey neck bobbed. "There's this group of multi-national communications corporations. They are major stakeholders in the Caribbean. The group believes the basin will become a pivotal area of the world. They're looking for someone with experience, loyalty, integrity, and courage. I told them to look no further than Al Crist. They already knew about you . . . as a Pulitzer Prize journalist."

Al remembered not understanding what Doc was offering at first. All he could see was the peaceful Caribbean and himself dying of perfect boredom. "Why me? My integrity's more than up for questioning."

"But, they don't know that, now do they, lad?"

"No, Doc. I guess not."

"As far as they know, you've got what they need, and they're willing to provide you with a five-year contract--six figures plus royalties and you'll have a villa by the sea and a motor yacht equipped with all the modern communications gadgets. You know, computers, modems, cellular phone connections, and the rest. I don't understand all this modern gadgetry." He paused and smiled without showing his teeth. "Have you ever had an offer like that before, lad? Have you?"

"No."

"I'd act as your Control . . . your primary contact that is. Just like it's been all these years anyway. You'd just be working for a bunch of rich and powerful communications conglomerates rather than the one and only Company."

"So, what's the catch, Doc?"

"No catch. Just the opportunity of two lifetimes, lad. Look, the instincts of some very powerful and savvy people are that the Caribbean is about ready to erupt again. CARICOM's been too quiet. Castro's been invisible. Everything's been too quiet and invisible. And, the good old U S of A has not been overly successful in that region as you know. Kennedy tried with the Alliance for Progress. It just made things worse by Americanizing the Caribbean more and fostering a welfare mentality in many areas. That Caribbean seemed to beg for Johnson's gunboat diplomacy. Reagan seemed to like that approach also, but he added economic recovery back in from the Kennedy days. The results: Reagan's Caribbean Basin Initiative and the invasion of Grenada. Then, we 'save' Haiti from itself." He made quote marks in the air with his hands as he said the word save. "Even whatever it is you're doing down in--where is it? Belize or something?--probably relates to this whole Caribbean thing. The consortium thinks that the area is a volcano waiting to erupt. They--and I--want you down there to report on it when it happens and everything leading up to it."

"Not to influence what happens, right? Just report it, right?"

"No Company stuff, lad. Just do your journalism thing. That's what they want from you and me."

* * * * *

"Eloise Anselm-Smith. Eloise Anselm-Smith. Please come to the Eastern Airlines information desk." The deep voice with a Spanish accent blasted from overhead loudspeakers throughout the Miami International Airport. "Eloise Anselm-Smith. Por favor, Eastern Airlines informacion."

Lois reached with the immaculate crimson nails of her left hand for the lock of hair that always drooped over her forehead when she began to feel hassled. But it wasn't there. The perm. She'd completely forgotten about that damned perm. Her luxurious Afro-style ringlets were somewhere between auburn and jet black depending upon how the light struck them. She just wasn't used to these curls yet. People from all over the Caribbean and the world brushed passed her like harsh whispers, together creating a buzzing roar of humanity in English and Spanish and French and German

8

and fourteen zillion other languages not unlike the milieu she was used to and thrived in--The City.

"Eloise Anselm-Smith. Please come to the Eastern Airlines information desk."

She stretched her legs just slightly in spite of her solemn resolve when she had sashayed out of her suite of offices overlooking The Avenue of the Americas just four hours ago to let nothing hurry her for the next three months. She'd be arriving in St. Thomas just three days before Carnival. And, for three delicious months, she was going to develop a golden Caribbean tan, eat lots of seafood, and drink lots of island rum. Maybe she'd even get lucky. It *had* been a long time.

So, what on earth could it be now? Just like it had been for the past four relentless years, somebody or something was depending upon her for a decision, for some action. That was how she'd gotten *Mystique* off the ground and nursed it into a full-blown international publication to be reckoned with. All the experts had declared her demise before she ever printed the first edition of her combination fashion and politics monthly. Not only was a magazine risky at best, but a magazine that combined fashion and politics? It just wasn't the kind of book that would fly. And a former Ms. World jock at the helm? Gimme a break! And she did get a break. It was called the Internet.

She didn't give a damn then, and she sure as hell didn't give a damn now, what any of them thought. She'd been fresh off a stinking, demeaning divorce from a snail of a man whom she'd helped make into a snail before she'd realized what they were both doing. She'd tried to apologize, to make amends. Howard Smith, her ex, had thought that she'd gone insane. But what had happened was that they had gone inane. She left him on the spot . . . taking her toothbrush and an old Navy pea coat from her hippie days at Radcliffe that she'd saved for some reason she had never been able to uncover. She'd even carried that damned toothbrush through every competition as if it were some kind of totem. It had been her good luck and her bad luck. It had been her luck.

That was not, however, all she settled for when the divorce proceedings began. She figured that she'd stayed home and sacrificed her later career potential to be his maid, his harlot, his hostess, his bait or whatever else he'd needed her for, to build that goddamned management consulting firm of his which had turned him into the snail he was when she left him. Well, he

9

was making a killing, and she had figured (and her lawyer agreed) that she should at least have the chance to make a go of it in her own business if that was really what she wanted to do, without having to use up what little she'd been able to save during her bodybuilding competition days before their marriage. That was all the non-marital assets she had. After all, one of the conditions of the marriage was that she give up her career. Finally, after months of pretty seedy negotiations between their lawyers, a one-shot settlement was agreed to. "Lump sum," her lawyer called it. No monthly alimony. Just the grubstake she thought she'd surely earned over their five years. Oh, Jesus! Had it really been only five years? It had seemed like so much longer.

The Eastern Information Counter stopped Lois in mid-stride. "Oh." She peeked up over the countertop glistening white and royal blue in the bright Miami International Airport. She couldn't decide if the light was artificial or somehow from the real sun outside. "Excuse me. I wasn't watching where I was walking." Lois felt herself flushing.

"May I help you?" The Latin supervisor leaned toward her over the counter, smiling. His even teeth glistened white in that same light.

"Ah . . . yes. I'm Eloise Anselm-Smith. You just paged me?"

"Oh . . . ?" The supervisor turned to another young man standing behind her with a question in his dark eyes. He seemed to be a clone of the supervisor.

"Si." He handed the supervisor a small piece of paper that the supervisor glanced at as he turned his black eyed-gaze back on her.

"Yes, Ms. Anselm-Smith. If you would go the end of this counter. See?"

"Yes?"

"No, not si. Look." He pointed to where the counter made a right angle turn to the left and seemed to disappear into a crowd of passengers waiting to go to the Dominican Republic. "There is a bank of blue-and-white telephones there. Your call is on number two."

Lois nodded. "Oh." She could feel the flush subsiding. "Thank you."

"De nada." He grinned.

She returned his smile, then bolted for the telephones.

10

"Thank you for flying Eastern."

Who could it be? It certainly wasn't Howard. Not after all that had happened between them. Hell, she hadn't even spoken to him in over six months, and, as far as she knew, he didn't have any idea she was going to St. Thomas for three months off. He only called when he did to see how badly she was doing. He'd expected her to fail. In fact, he'd even tried to tell her what to do with her settlement, just like he'd told her what to do with everything else in her life with him from sprinkling paprika on the deviled eggs or not to whether or not to take yoga on Tuesday and Thursday afternoons at two-thirty or on Monday and Wednesday evenings at six. Whether to have her own career or not. When she'd stood him down that morning in his Madison Avenue penthouse offices while they attempted to have an adult, civilized after-divorce-settlement brunch that she was going to invest in a magazine publishing venture, he broke down sobbing.

"I'm absolutely vindicated, do you hear?" His sobs had evolved into screams that she was throwing his hard-earned money down the proverbial publishing sewer. "Publishing a magazine on the Internet and in print. You *are* insane!"

"No, Howard. I'm a publisher."

"What's the difference?"

Ignoring his remark, she had reached into her handbag and scooped out the brass-with-black-lettering desk nameplate she'd bought that very morning. "And I've got the name plate to prove it!" She'd grinned and shoved it at his face, which collapsed with disbelief.

"Do you suppose, Eloise, that all one needs to become transformed from a weight lifter to a successful publisher is a little capital from one's divorce settlement and a desk plate with one's name followed by the word publisher printed on it?"

"Engraved," she had corrected. "That's what the lettering is, Howard . . . engraved!"

She scowled now remembering that ugly morning and Howard's silly desperate slurs on her abilities and intelligence. She remembered emphasizing to him that she was sure all one needed was a little money and a desk plate to become successful at anything. "After all, Howard, look at you."

That had gored the unsuspecting picador more than he had wanted to let on. By the time she'd left his offices that morning, Lois was sure of one thing. Her stupid ex-husband knew she was just as capable of drawing blood as any other bastard trying to make a go of it. And he could add that to her grub stake and desk plate.

Damn! Who would be calling her way down here in Miami . . . now, just before she was to take off on a very long, very deserved, and very much needed sun-soaked vacation in the American Paradise . . . the Virgin Islands? All she knew was that if someone hadn't died or needed suicide counseling or something; she was going to be hard to deal with. After more than four years without a day off from that magazine--not even weekends, not even cocktail parties or dinner. Shit! It was like being a doctor or a shrink (well, psychiatrists were doctors too, weren't they?).

"What am I saying?" she laughed to herself. "Was? It is still like that. Here I am going to answer a call right now, probably to talk to someone in New York and most likely someone from my office with some problem they are convinced only I can handle." She knew she was muttering again. It was a bad habit that one seemed to pick up living alone. She knew also that she needed to watch herself. Muttering people weren't what one would call the most credible people around.

Lois sucked in a deep breath as she shoved through the crowd of Spanish-speaking passengers clustered near the telephones waiting to hear about their delayed flight. It seemed like all the flights were delayed this afternoon. Phone number two was at the far end of the telephone bank. She felt the coolness of the royal blue receiver in her hand as she picked it up and tucked it under her day-old perm to her right ear. "Eloise here."

"Lois, honey. So glad I caught you before you took off for paradise."

"Doc?"

"Yes, honey. Old Doc Streeter here."

There was a hissing silence on the line. Even though Doc had lived in the City for years, he still called everybody "honey" just as he was raised to back in North Carolina.

"So sorry to bother you now, honey, but I missed you at your office."

"What's up, Doc?" she laughed. It was their own little inside joke.

"I need your help with something, Lois."

12

"Sure, Doc. Anything for you. You know that."

"Good. I was hoping I could count on you, honey."

"What do you need, Doc?"

"An envelope will be hand-delivered to you at your boarding gate. I want you to deliver it to my associate in St. Thomas. You've used a lot of his material in your book."

"Oh?"

"Yes. And he fills your web site with blood and gore that evokes pity and sympathy. You've heard me speak of him often. Alfred Crist?"

"Yes. Crist. He's your Caribbean expert."

"And *your* cover story about five times, honey. That's the lad."

"Well, sure, I can do that."

"The message inside is very confidential, Lois. I don't want even you to read it. But I want you to guard it carefully. Okay?"

"Sure, Doc. Whatever you say."

"Just make damned sure he gets that envelop as soon as you reach St. Thomas. Call him from the airplane to meet you at the airport. I've tried to reach him, but the lines have been really tied up for some reason." Doc Streeter paused. "Of course, that's not the first time the telephone lines in the islands have been screwed up."

Lois could hear him breathing heavily on the other end of the line through the static. He always did that when he was excited or agitated.

"His number is area code 809, 776-9999. You got that, honey?"

"You know once I hear a number I've got it?"

"I know. But humor me?"

"809-776-9999."

"Okay, good. Listen, honey, I can't emphasize enough the importance of what's in that envelope. It may literally be a matter of life and death for some people, okay?"

She sighed.

"I don't mean that you'll be in any danger, honey. You'll be perfectly safe. The only people who will even know you are carrying this envelope for me will be you, me, and the Cuban airport maintenance man who will give you the envelope just outside of your boarding gate.

"Yes, Doc. It's very important that this Alfred Crist get the envelope and that the confidentiality of its contents be kept in tact, but I am not in any kind of personal danger."

"Good, honey. Good!"

"Anything else, Doc?"

"No, that's quite enough, I think," he chuckled. "Just enjoy your well-earned vacation. I'll keep an eye on the book while you're gone, honey."

"Thanks, Doc. Hell, if it weren't for you, there wouldn't be any book at all."

"Not so, honey. Not so at all. I just gave you a few little boosts here and there when you needed them. You've made that book into what it is through your ass-busting work."

"Thanks, Doc. I need to hear that right now. It's like leaving my new-born baby, you know?"

"Yes, I know."

"Okay, Doc. Gotta catch my flight . . . and pick up your package."

"Have fun, honey. Maybe Crist can show you around. He knows those islands better than just about anybody . . . and he's got this great yacht . . . *Remembrance of Things Past.*"

"Proust, huh? Well, maybe."

"Thanks again, Lois. Have a good time in American Paradise. Give my best to the lad."

"Okay. Thanks, Doc. See you in three months."

"See you, honey."

Lois hung up the telephone and proceeded to wade back through the pack of waiting passengers toward concourse B, gate ten. Jesus, she hadn't even left the airport yet and she was already involved in some kind of intrigue. This could prove to be a more interesting trip than she might ever have imagined.

* * * * *

Time does have a way of getting by you here, Al thought as he gradually moved toward the surface and the red warning buoy. Not just beneath the surface of the ocean where the elk horn, brain, and other coral formations clustered around crevices and caverns hiding lobsters and moray eels but also up on the surface as well. Time moves as surreptitiously as a good agent, as a current sweeping through the depths of the sea. It slithers through the seasons which are so similar to each other that you have to be very aware of signs, such as the flamboyants blooming, or century plants sprouting their giant flower pods that were used by many islanders as Christmas trees. That did make it a little tough to keep track of time passing.

At twenty-five feet, Al glanced off to his right. That nurse shark he speared lolled in a vortex of its own blood just below the surface several hundred feet away. Teddy's kill was a hundred feet or so closer. The short spears in each shark protruded slightly out of the water, gleaming in the sunlight of a late April day. Al breathed a little deeper with relief . . . no other sharks had yet been attracted by the bleeding targets. Hell, he mused, if they really were Thomian sharks, then it would take them a while to get here anyway. He held at the twenty-five foot level, waiting for Teddy to move on up. He was still staring at the sharks, shaking his head in amazement and relief that both of their shots had hit the mark from such distances. The Feds would sure as hell be pleased with these results.

Now that the attacks were history, Al figured that Teddy must be dreaming of shark steaks. Their plan was to head out for the Atlantic side of the island after spearing their sharks to find a cove with a little beach and some reef. They'd catch a few grouper or snapper, snare some lobsters, and build a huge fire on the beach. Frenchie would cook as usual since he was far and away the best at it. A feast! That's what they had to look forward to. They'd sleep overnight on the beach rather than going back to the yacht. Being boys again. That was what it was all about. They seemed to need it sometimes. That and hiding out until they could figure out what was going on with the threats on his life. But, as he watched Teddy turn his masked face away from the sharks and back toward the direction of the red buoy, Al felt sure that all of what he and Frenchie had planned was going to become the victim of the red buoy.

Rested, Teddy Morhead swam on toward the surface. Al followed, Doc Streeter's words still ringing in his ears as if he were hearing them while he swam behind the Virgin Islands Senate President.

"The United States Virgin Islands, lad. Think of it! At your age, you get to live in the American Paradise." Doc had ruffled the white tumble of curls that collapsed just around his button-down collar. With his slightly balding crown, his hair gave the appearance of a lion's mane. "At least, that's what the license plates say."

Doc had always seemed to understand him better than most, Al had to admit. And he sure busted his ass to get Al that Mexico City assignment so he could get away from all that cultural revolution craziness after Kent State. He just couldn't take it anymore. That could've been the beginning of the end for his journalism career right then and there. He just needed to get as much distance as he could between him and that shit as the world of his work would allow. Old Doc seemed to understand. To this day, Al didn't know how or why, but he did. And he put his own frigging job on the line just to get him that transfer. Al was so junior with UPI that he would not normally have been considered for such an assignment so soon, but Doc had told them that either they give the lad the job or he would walk too. Of course, Al didn't know anything about Doc's actions until years later when they got drunk together one night in a Kuala Lumpur bar and got to talking about the past. It just sort of sneaked out of him after about his fourth or tenth gin and tonic

"No catch, lad." He remembered Doc's steel eyes actually smiling as he repeated the point for emphasis.

"Jesus, Doc. What do you mean there's no catch? If you could just look in the mirror, Doc, and see your own steel eyes that have never smiled in all the years I've known you just smiling away."

"Well," Doc began. He almost broke down laughing before he could continue. "Well . . . I guess you've sort of got me, lad."

"I just knew it."

"Yeah. The catch is that this assignment is for the duration, and it's in paradise."

16

* * * * *

The 727 screamed into the one hundred percent humidity of a Miami April afternoon. Lois clasped her tan calfskin briefcase between her high heels. Inside it, Doc Streeter's nine by twelve manila envelope teased her journalistic curiosity. She really wanted to know what it contained, but she'd promised Doc not to look.

The Cuban maintenance attendant who gave her the envelope had cautioned her again, his bluish lips curled around an unlit, half-burned cigar. "Keep it safe . . . and do not look inside, Senorita."

So she didn't, even after the seatbelt sign was turned off and she wedged her briefcase between her and the window on her right. Somehow, she believed, that squirrelly little Cuban man with the craters covering his cheeks was still watching her.

Outside the window beneath a spotty covering of wispy white clouds, Miami transformed from a crowded sprawling city into a mirage of distant canals and blocks of tiny buildings with coral roofs and miniature vehicles scooting along ribbons of concrete and asphalt. Less than three hours away was paradise.

She was really proud of her restraint so far, but she didn't know if it would last the entire flight. Doc Streeter had been a good friend over the years, more like the father she never had than anything else. He just seemed to be that sort of man. From what she could tell, he'd been a lot the same way with mister ace war correspondent, Pulitzer Prize winner, and now Caribbean expert for the entire news world, Alfred Crist. She really liked his work, but for some reason she couldn't quite put her finger on, she seemed predisposed to dislike him. Maybe it could be put off to some sort of pseudo-sibling rivalry since they were both Doc's children in one way or another.

She first met Doc at a cocktail party at Radcliffe several years before she'd begun bodybuilding competition and before she'd even met Howard. She often thought later on, after her marriage was going down hill faster than Franz Klammer, that she should've married Doc. But he wasn't the marrying kind. She sensed that even naive and nineteen under the influence of several very dry Bombay martinis. He'd come to the school as a writer-in-residence for six weeks. The cocktail party was given in his honor the

17

evening after his first presentation on journalism and the new world of fact and fiction. He'd tried to demonstrate some kind of connection between the Tom Wolf type of new journalism fiction in books like "Electric Kool Aid Acid Test" and the old journalism of reporting so-called actual facts. As she remembered, he really made a pretty good stab at tearing down their preconceived ideas of fiction and fact, of reporting and creating, by allowing them to crawl inside of his mind as he opened it up through repeated references to his book on Vietnam which he claimed was based entirely on what they would normally call facts but was in fact a complete fiction.

Lois remembered being absolutely in awe, as in love, with that disheveled, graying goose of a man who continually pulled at his left ear lobe as if it were a trigger for his brain and who nearly always seemed to say the right thing at the wrong time at cocktail parties. He even seemed somewhat insecure and shy around all the mini-skirted Radcliffe girls who surrounded him from the time he walked into the elegant home of her journalism professor and slugged down his first two Glenfidiches before even sampling the gourmet buffet laid out for the occasion.

"Somet'ing to drink, ma'am?"

"Oh, yes. Thank you."

"What will dat be, ma'am?" The stewardess's low-pitched voice had that distinctive Caribbean lilt she'd heard on commercials.

"White wine."

"To be sure, ma'am." The stewardess bent over her cart to retrieve a white wine miniature.

"On second thought, do you have any of that island rum?"

"We have Cruzan, ma'am. Made in St. Croix." She smiled. "Gold or light?"

"Which do you prefer?"

"Gold, ma'am. It's much smoother . . . almost like a good scotch."

"Good. Let me have two gold rums, some ice, and a coke."

The stewardess sucked her teeth.

"No coke?"

"I don' t'ink you'll be needing dat, ma'am."

"Okay." She shrugged. "Why not."

"Lime with dat, ma'am?"

Lois studied the stewardess's caramel face. She could read nothing on it's smooth, clear features, so she took a chance. "Yes?"

"Yes," she nodded. "Yes, ma'am."

"Thanks."

The stewardess turned to move to the next line of seats. She paused, turning back toward Lois. "You be goin' to St. Thomas for Carnival, ma'am?"

Lois nodded. "Yes. And, I'll be there for three whole months after that."

"Dat's wonderful, ma'am. To be sure, you enjoy de Carnival parade. De people all be dressed up in deir costumes and t'ing and singin' and playin' de best calypsos of de year. But, most of all, don' miss de J'Ouvert morning tramp, ma'am, before de parade. De people trampin' by torchlight to de music of de bands . . . dat be somet'ing, mon . . . ah, ma'am."

"I'm sure I'll enjoy it all. Ah." Lois flushed a little. "T'anks, mon."

As she popped the top on the second golden Cruzan and poured it over her second cup of ice already partially melted even in the extremely cool air-conditioned environment of the 727, all resolve faded. She unzipped her brief and extracted the manila envelope. She examined it for several moments as if looking for a way in without breaking the seal. Then she shrugged her shoulders and tore it open. Inside was another manila envelope with a typed note attached.

> Knew your journalistic curiosity would
> get you this far, honey. But please don't
> go any further. This could be the biggest
> breaking story of the decade! If Crist wants
> to let you in on it early, so your book gets
> an exclusive, so much the better. But leave
> it to his judgment, okay? We're talking
> national security, honey!

19

Love you,

Doc

Damn! Lois punched the call button above her head. He knew her just too well, now didn't he? But, she knew, too, that she'd respect his wishes even if it killed her.

"Yes, ma'am?"

"I'll need a telephone as soon as we get close enough to St. Thomas to use it."

"Oh, yes, ma'am. In about twenty minutes?"

"Thank you."

"You're very welcome, ma'am." The stewardess smiled. "Is dere anyt'ing else?"

"No, thank you."

"Twenty minutes." She pivoted and glided toward the rear of the aircraft.

Lois pulled the note off the envelope and placed the manila tempter back into her brief, zipping it closed. This time she knew it was for the last time until she gave up the contents to Alfred Crist.

* * * * *

The cool blue sea warmed as they approached the surface. Doc's words still bounced around in his head. "The duration? That's however long it takes for you to find out what's going down in the Caribbean, if anything, and who's behind it."

"We want guts-ball features of the kind you're noted for, lad.   Hard news about political, social, and important criminal activities and situations.

"And you are definitely the man for the job, lad. There's no doubt in my mind, and there's no doubt in the minds of those who have come to me seeking my help in finding the best journalist for the job.

20

"What the hell, lad! Bikini-clad, tanned young ladies all year long . . . vacation weather all de time, mon." Doc raised his hands above his head and snapped his fingers in time to some calypso he heard in his mind.

"Well, Doc. Since you put it like that, and you've already pulled me out of the best little war we've had going lately."

"Which is your own twisted version of paradise, I take it?" Doc teased.

Al could not help but chuckle at that comment. Nam had made him a good bit more sanguine than the average guy. Doc Streeter was one of the few people in the world who really seemed to understand it and how it had motivated him over the years to remain in conflict areas to do his work . . . his best work.

"But, I just don't know, Doc! The whole thing stinks of Company . . . and that sounds pretty much like a catch to me."

"What do you mean, lad?"

"You know I'm not going to be some shill for a bunch of rich, powerful, overreaching bastards who want to control the world like the Trilateral Commission or the Council on Foreign Relations or the Company!"

"For Christ sake, lad! Just this once will you cool your young ass out and give old Doc Streeter a chance to finish? Will you?"

Al turned sharply from Doc's probing eyes, almost turning his back on the table. "Okay . . . okay. I'm still listening." He stifled a laugh. "Barely."

"Oh you are such a smart ass, lad."

"I know."

"Look, you'd work independently. You'd have to resign from the book of course."

"That's the least of the problems."

"The people I'm working with are owners and major stock holders of the top media corporations in the world--print and electronic and Internet. You would contribute dispatches, articles, and a series now and again to their various publications and news services around the world like our old alma maters UPI and Time. Even radio and TV, lad. You'll become a media star. The exposure will be, simply put, phenomenal!"

"I don't know." Al turned about halfway back toward the small conference table with the late morning sun reflecting in the wax shine on its myrtle surface, but he continued to gaze out the window of Doc's office overlooking the spires of glass and steel that were New York.

"I know it'll be hard to take, lad, but you'll be very high profile so you'll have to live a very good lifestyle. You'll have a very righteous lifestyle, lad. A motor yacht, a seaside villa with private docking, a pool and hot tub, and most importantly a bottomless bank account for the full term of the initial contract which will be five years. If you make the full five-year contract and performed well, you will get everything free and clear as a bonus. At that time, we would determine whether it was valuable to enter into another contract.

"Lad, this is very big! So big that I'd do it myself if I could. At my age, unfortunately, the strength and stamina needed for this kind of assignment just aren't available to me anymore. Nor is the genius for political investigation and analysis that you possess. Then again, I never did have that . . . come to think of it . . . at any age." "Lad, it means all the money and luxury and opportunity you'll ever desire. And, most important, it means probably the best damned opportunity you'll ever have to work at what you love the most and do it with as few constraints and as much freedom of journalistic and investigative spirit as you could ever hope for. You'll be set for life, lad. Set for life!"

The sea splashed open around them. Al remembered that when he had still hesitated, Doc's face and bald spot turned purple as he mumbled, "Well, I didn't want to resort to this, lad. But you leave me no choice." He cleared his turkey throat. "You see, this whole scheme was cooked up by one Juan Santurce, the new Assistant Secretary of the Interior for Territorial Affairs. He wants somebody out in the front yard, lad, to keep an eye on things. Somebody he can trust. He particularly contacted me because I am your boss and confidant."

"Santurce. Shit!"

"He wants me to release you from your contract here but still be your primary contact while you're on the assignment. Everything else I told you is true. Santurce figured that setting this up through a private consortium

22

would be the best way to go." Doc fidgeted with his glasses. "He has even more faith in you than I do."

"I didn't think that was possible, Doc." Al winked. "Better get those damned glasses adjusted."

"And, he says you are responsible for him . . . that you owe him."

So, because what Doc Streeter said about Juan Santurce was true, Frenchie now stood above Al astride the teak deck of Remembrance of Things Past waving his stubby sunburned arms wildly as Al pushed Teddy up onto the ladder toward the main deck. Coming out of the water with those tanks and flippers on could be a real shaky experience at times.

Al felt the suction pulling at his cheeks and releasing as he ripped his mask away from his face and seated it on the top of his head. "Frenchie! Get your arms around Teddy, mon, instead of waving them all over the deck like palm trees in a blow."

Without a word, Frenchie jumped to on the deck of the sixty-five foot Taiwan-crafted classic beauty with twin Perkins engines which his friend and skipper had named after a Marcel Proust novel . . . whatever that was. First, he snatched Teddy's spear gun, quickly stowing it nearby. Then he grabbed hold gingerly of the Senate President Theodore V. Morhead and pulled him onto the teak deck, air tanks and all, as if he were a child, which he certainly was not.

Teddy Morhead was a towering man of six feet seven inches, weighing in at two hundred and ten pounds, and he was still in just about as good a shape as he was when he played forward for the Boston Celtics until three years ago. He had been voted all-pro four times in nine years of active professional basketball. But, bad knees and a bad conscience about getting home and helping out his islands shortened his career years ahead of schedule.

Frenchie's weather beaten and somewhat knurled body was deceptive, as were the Sea Grape trees, which his body often reminded Al of. Al knew just how deceptive too. He, himself, could bench press a hundred and thirty pounds for considerable reps. And old Frenchie Bryan could wrench a line out of his hands with ease. Sometimes they would have contests. The loser had to cook or clean the catch or whatever else had to be done for the day when they were out sailing. Usually, the contest was standing on opposite sides of the helm, each of them trying to force the yacht to his heading.

23

Frenchie loved these contests of strength because he always won so he got out of doing a lot of work that he was already getting paid for. What the hell! Al laughed to himself. What are friends for anyway? That was Frenchie. He appeared bent and knurled but was stronger than a frigging hurricane . . . a veritable Sea Grape tree.

"Cap'n?"

"Yo, Frenchie?" Al shed his tanks and yanked his mask off the top of his head while he kicked off his flippers. He wore no wet suit.

Frenchie took a deep gulp of air as he always did when he was overly excited about something. "Call for you from your message service, me son." His flat white face, burned brown-red by the continual exposure to the sun over the past sixty-three years in the islands and at sea, was flushed. "Some woman, she call from da airplane. She say she have an urgent message for you from Doc Streeter."

"Who is she? When did she call?"

"I go'tit all wrote down, Cap'n. In da Wheelhouse."

CHAPTER 2
WEST END COMMUNE

The two Grenadians who approached the Ujamma Commune grounds in their jeep along the main cart path wore their hair in locks, but they were not Rastafari. They did not sit erect in their bucket seats as the jeep bounced between towering mahogany trees and through thick foliage which continually grew back over the path no matter how many times a machete was taken to it, past the gate opening and into the center of the living quarters section of the compound surrounded by the rocks and trees of the east end of the island. What these two men did do was to not realize that no motor-driven vehicles were allowed on the commune grounds of the Rastafarian family of Ras Ujamma I.

"Mo-tor driv-en con-trap-tions be de work of de con-ti-nen-tal devils!" Ras Ujamma I preached in his sharp voice heavy with a Bajan twang not unlike the old Pirate's brogue that could cut your eardrums like a razor. "If we use deir inventions, den we sure as Jah become like dem . . . ci-ti-zens of Ba-by-lon . . .!" Driving, even riding in, motor vehicles was forbidden. These Rastas walked or ran everywhere they went . . . except, of course, when one of them had to travel to St. John or St. Croix or even further to Jamaica or the States. Rasta brothers and sisters would partake of great meditation in the form of smoking huge quantities of ganja for days prior to such a flight or sail.

When the two men alighted from their jeep, one was even more positive that they were not Rastafari. Rastafari stood erect, shoulders straight and walked with a strong steady stride. These Grenadians walked slumped forward, their shoulders hunched towards their chests almost as if they were bent over by the weight of the moment. The trees seemed sentinels in the early morning light.

Edna Black was the first person in the compound to encounter the strangers. She'd heard engine noises as she lay in her bed half awake, half asleep, thinking about depositions and evidentiary hearings relating to two Rasta brothers busted yesterday for pot. Ras I had summoned her to the commune to discuss their case. "Get that jeep out of here!" She couldn't believe anybody actually had driven into Ras Ujamma I's compound. "Now!"

"Wha' . . .."

"We jus' be comin' to see de mon, girl."

"Ras Ujamma I, girl."

"All the more reason to get that goddamned jeep out of this compound . . . post haste, mon!"

Reluctantly, the two Grenadians retreated toward their jeep, routed by a woman. They were perplexed at this woman of startling beauty like a model on the cover of *Ebony* but sleeping in a Rasta commune, this woman possessed of such a direct and willful nature that they could not tear their eyes from hers.

"Ras Ujamma I has prohibited motor-driven vehicles, electricity, public water, any food other than organic, and Walkman radios here at the commune."

"We didn' know."

"Really, Miss . . . ah."

"Really?" She had to turn her face away, back toward the shanty reserved for her when she stayed over, to avoid laughing in their faces.

"Really . . . yes, really . . . Miss . . . ah."

"Attorney." She pivoted back toward this West Indian version of Dogberry and Verges. "Attorney Edna Black."

The two men stumbled into their jeep and backed it out of the compound into the cover of the jungle-like growth, which dominated this western end of St. Thomas. Their intelligence sources had identified Ras I as the most likely person to install as the surrogate leader. Their sources told them to come early because Ras I was an early riser and respected early-morning business. But they had not informed them about this prohibition of motor vehicles or about Attorney Edna Black.

They had been told, however, to bring appropriate gifts for Ras I. He was respected, even by his political enemies, because he was perceived to be a man of integrity. So as they returned to the compound on foot, they carried backpacks stuffed with pounds of the very best Colombian gold sensimilla for this mystic leader and his following.

"Guess de reports dat dis Ras I mon be a fanatical be true, Fist," Slider whispered as they re-entered the compound.

"Yes, mon. Cyan be hard, hard, hard to get him outta dat."

"Yes, mon. But he cyanno' be leader of an emergin' island nation livin' like dis." Slider swept his arms about him to signify the compound. "He must be adaptin'."

* * * * *

"Gentlemen." Ras Ujamma I smiled beatifically. "I and I presume you may be addressed in dat manner?"

"Ras Ujamma I," the two men dueted, then stopped and glared at each other.

"Ras Ujamma I," the short red-skinned leader of the pair tentatively began again, this time alone. "We bring you greetings from de USMC."

"No, mon? De two of you be marines?" Smile wrinkles erupted around his nearly black eyes.

"No, mon. No. We bring you greetings from de United Separatist Movement of the Caribbean . . . USMC . . ." he smiled back, "and we bring you a fine gift of de most superb sensimilla herb grown right here in de Caribbean for you and your family here." He swept a knurled hand toward the opening in the shack. Then he nudged his slender and slightly taller partner, who promptly began dumping foot and two-foot-long blond tops onto the woven palm mat between them on the dirt floor. The golden tops glowed in the soft lantern light. "I be Slider. My partner, here, be known as Fist because of his knowledge of de martial arts."

"And where do Slider come from, Slider?" Ras I chuckled. "From your ability to slide in and out of situations . . .?"

"Something like dat." He smirked, trying to imitate Edna Black's earlier smirk.

"We be startin' de greatest coup in de history of de Caribbean." Fist stopped short as if something had caught in his throat. He glanced sheepishly at Slider as if he might have spoken out of turn.

27

Ras I noticed the exchange of glances. "A real live revolution, mesons?"

"Uniforms . . . guns . . . jeeps." Slider sputtered. "No. No jeeps unless you want dem, of course," he grinned and picked between his teeth with a stem of a two-foot-long amber bud caked with resin supersaturated with THC. "And we have full-fledged, honest-to-comrade C-rations from de American National Guard!"

Fist clenched his fist and shoved it at the roof of the palm frond hut much in the manner of a shot putter's motion when putting the shot. "Coup de uber alles! Coup de uber alles!"

Edna turned her head from them to hide the laughter tearing at the edges of her lips. She never could figure out how Ras I could keep such an inscrutable face, even in the face of this. She knew she sure couldn't. For a change, she was quite happy that there was only natural light in the hut. That made it a lot easier for her to hide her struggle with laughter.

"We really need your help, Ras Ujamma I," Slider stroked. "We already have all your renegades enlisted. We be poised and ready to strike."

Fist nodded as his chorus.

"And we need only the right leader to run dese islands after we take over. We need *your* leadership to finally take control of what be ours!"

"Coup de uber alles!"

"Not now, Fist." Slider winced. "Not now!"

For the first time, Fist glared at Slider as if Slider had made some kind of mistake.

"Why don't you roll us up one of your famous blimpie spliffs, mon?"

Fist nodded. He bent over the woven palm mat and immediately began the ordered task of rolling a giant spliff.

"We've put out t'reat notes to de Governor and Senate President. By dis afternoon, dey will know dat dey will be assassinated at Carnival if dey don' capitulate. We goin' to destroy de capitalist-backed leadership in dese islands and return de power to de people."

"Despite the collapse of communism around the world?" Edna

smirked.

Slider froze. He fired up the spliff Fist shoved at him and inhaled deeply trying not to glare at Edna Black. He wanted to ignore her if he could. "If you and your family here want to lead after our revolution is successful, den you mus' be willing to get involved now . . . to commit yourself now!" Slider shrugged, almost apologetically. "And who cares a damn, mon, for what white people in foreign parts of de world be doing, me-son . . .? Dey got not'ing to do wit' we, mon!"

"But what you are askin' I and I to do, Mr. Slider, be not in de natural flow of t'ings, mon. I and I *be* committed, mon . . . to au naturale."

"According to America's own Thomas Jefferson, it be natural for de people to rise up against any government dat has betrayed its social contract wit' de people. Dis government in dese islands be tramplin' all over its contract with our people! I know dat! You know dat! All o' we know dat!"

"But guns, planes, ships . . . and jeeps," Ras chuckled a little. "Dey destroy nature! De nature I and I be absolutely committed to preservin'!"

"I and I jus' not be convinced as to how a religious farmer and his family can arguably get involved with dis gambit of yours wit'out givin' up much too much personally . . . you know what I and I mean?" Ras I paused, while the two gentlemen from Grenada stared at each other with obeah eyes, digesting his change to nearly impeccable English. "Ethically?"

"Oh, yes, mon," Slider fielded. "Certainly we do."

"What be natural," Fist sorted out on his own, "be . . . ah . . . be, ah, defined by de times, isn't it?"

The spliff was burning like a chimney. Smoke swirled upward, thick sweet ganja smoke, coiling around their circle. The four of them sat cross-legged around a palm mat woven by the Coconut Man from Dominica inside a woven palm hut built by Rastas on the island of St. Thomas in the U.S. Virgin Islands purchased from the Danes by the United States in 1917 for $25,000,000. The spliff came to Ras I from Edna Black's perfumed hands that were so soft when she would let them be . . . those hands . . . that odor which excited him beyond his own understanding . . . it was not natural either . . . that smell. He saw her nod twice . . . that was one of their signals. "I and I t'ink abou'tit, gentlemen." Ras closed his eyes, sucked the

29

golden Colombian smoke deep into his well-conditioned lungs until his chest would not expand any further and the scilliae tingled. The rich smoke languored about his dread locks like an aura.

"He'll think about it," Edna shot at them from very close range. She stood, motioning to them to do the same as she glided toward the doorway of the hut.

"You better t'ink fast, Ras Ujamma I, if you wan' be in power when de time comes . . . not out!" Fist surprised himself and everyone else by getting through the entire sentence without a noticeable error.

"We've started our attack plan as of dis mornin' on de high seas. Right here, off de coast of St. Thomas! We be high-jackin' a world-famous journalist noted for his humanity and liberalism as well as his expertise on just what we be doin' . . . revolution. He will write stories for we, telling de world what all o' we wan' dem to hear, to read! He'll be makin' favorable world opinion of our revolution!"

"Coup de uber alles!" Fist cursed as he sucked on what was left of the spliff like he would've a bottle of Myers rum.

"Our revolution for freedom has begun, but it can still be yours too! It can still be led by de great and wise Ras Ujamma I and his Rastafarian family. Dis journalist we will have in our possession has many awards to his credit. He has, himself, been a soldier, a veteran of de Vietnam fiasco. He will be believed by de world. He will help us get aid from bot' sides. We shall rule de Caribbean!"

"Coup de uber alles!"

Ras I glanced at his lawyer and sometimes lover. He could not miss the fire in her eyes at the mention of the journalist these men bragged they were in the process of capturing on the high seas. "Might I inquire as to who dis journalist be, gentlemen?"

"Certainly." Slider spoke each syllable as if it were a word. "You have a right to know who be workin' for your movement." Slider paused while Ras I took a final hit off the smoldering spliff. "De journalist in question be . . . well, dere only be one such journalist in all of de Caribbean, Ras Ujamma I . . . Ms. Black. Dat be Alfred Crist."

30

CHAPTER 3

BATTLE ON THE HIGH SEAS

"Cap'n!"

"Yo, Frenchie?"

"On deck, Cap'n. Check dis out, me son!"

Al stumbled up the wooden ladder from his cabin to the Wheelhouse. The sun blazed like a flash bulb, blinding him for a moment. "What's going on, Frenchie?"

"Look to starboard, Cap'n! To starboard!" Frenchie's finger pointed toward the horizon. Al rubbed his eyes, trying to clear them of the flashbulb like spots floating around him. "Byoats, Cap'n. Alota byoats."

"Should we employ our new program?"

"Me-son. De computer already sayin' dere's an armed fleet out dere."

"Then, I guess we should."

"Already engaged, Cap'n."

Through the binoculars, Al could see a battleship gray trawler leading a small armada bearing down on *Remembrance of Things Past* at about ten knots per hour. Behind the ominous trawler, three custom Bertrams planed the trawler's shallow swells. Four forty-two foot cabin style cruisers plowed the same swells. Two cigarettes flanked the flotilla in front of the trawler.

For the first time, Al was thankful that Frenchie had practically forced him into allowing the arming and fortifying of Remembrance only a few months before. Frenchie had argued that they traveled throughout the Caribbean, and pirates--sometimes even governments--could present a real problem if they were unable to protect themselves if attacked. Al had to agree. Frenchie had been pestering Al for a shakedown cruise once he had everything installed. Being an old salt, he believed in shakedown cruises to get the kinks worked out. Only difference is this shakedown was under real life conditions . . . sort of like Frenchie's spear guns. Now, instead of spear guns against sharks it looked like Frenchie Bryan and company would be

31

testing his new weapons system for real against these guys bearing down on them . . . whoever the hell they were.

Ever since he had been a gunners mate in the Navy on the U.S. Lexington until it sank in the Battle of the Coral Sea and he and some Chief Fireman from North Carolina saved a Blue Jesus number of their own crew and the crews of two other vessels that went down almost at the exact same time by getting them all to makeshift rafts they fashioned out of rubble from the sinking ships and life preservers they salvaged from the dead and from the sea, Frenchie Bryan had had a love affair with weapons. As a Navy gunners mate, it was big guns he craved. But as a world class marksman and Olympic gold medal winner more than once during those same Navy years and for twenty-five years after the Navy mustered him out, Frenchie was the master of pistols and small bore rifles of all styles and caliber's. He liked to invent weapons as well, like the new super-powered spear gun they had just been testing out.

Frenchie claimed his crowning achievement to be the armament and weaponry system he had designed and installed personally on Remembrance after a heavy duty lobbying job on Al. His overwhelming argument was centered around only a single point--the yacht had recently been attacked by pirates. They'd just gone out for a limin' cruise . . . to get away from it all for a couple of days. They were attacked by three pirates off a scrubby motor sailor. Luckily, Remembrance was just too much boat for the pirates. Frenchie outmaneuvered the sluggish motor sailor, thus avoiding a boarding party which would have been pretty messy and, for sure, unpredictable as to outcome.

Once Al had agreed, Frenchie armed the vessel with twin M-60's in the bow and in the stern of the boat and a Gattling mini-gun on the fly bridge just like the ones in the "Puff the Magic Dragons" in Nam. He also put a small cannon on each side, amidship. Frenchie had wanted to install at least one rocket launcher, but Al had put his pocketbook down on that one. "This all has to stop somewhere, Frenchie, me-son," he had cackled. "And rocket launchers . . . well, rocket launchers is just going a little too far, mon."

All weapons were hidden inside the hull of Remembrance, which was protected by armor plating, as was the computer area beneath the Pilot's cabin. The Pilot's cabin itself held all the controls for the system and was protected by plating and glass that would withstand armor-piercing rockets according to the ad in "Soldier of Fortune." The Pilot's cabin also held a

32

complete arsenal of weapons from .38's and .357's to a grenade launcher and grenades.

"That's a helluva arsenal, me-son." Teddy tossed the AK-47 with the black tape on the stock handle that was nearly worn away with the years since its use to Al as requested. "I was a good Boy Scout," Al chuckled as he snatched his favorite weapon from the air. Some people . . . hell, most people . . . would just say it was his fight, not their's, so to hell with him. But not Al Crist. He was truly a friend . . . a friend to Teddy Morhead . . . and, more importantly, a friend to the Virgin Islands . . . and the Caribbean. And he'd proved that time and time again.

"Them be movin' in fast, Cap'n!"

The AK touched his fingers and palms in a familiar way, triggering instincts of years before. He locked and loaded the assault rifle. "Get the Thai Chi Sea Defense program going, Frenchie."

Frenchie smiled. "Already in place, Cap'n."

"Code the program to initiate action at will."

"Aye, Cap'n!" A series of keystrokes under Frenchie's cassava-like fingers filled the otherwise silent cabin.

* * * * *

Al's steel blue eyes searched for faces on the approaching vessels through the lenses of his binoculars. He did not want to unnecessarily hurt anyone or have any of his friends hurt or killed because of him. He wasn't casual about this at all. He simply knew that his computer had already identified the command center of the approaching armada, all weapons emplacements, as well as fuel and ammunition storage areas. The computer had, by now, prioritized each target in relation to other targets and assigned the destruction of each identified and prioritized target to a different sequence of weaponry bombardment combinations. He, Teddy, and Frenchie were armed more as a back up and to repel any attempts at boarding if they got close enough for that. Al counted three people on each cigarette. They were armed with assault rifles. M-60's were mounted in front of the windshields. They were beginning to fire across

33

Remembrance's bow as they passed. Their crews seemed to be the assault and boarding units.

The trawler was too dark to get a good look at who was on board even through the binoculars. The Bertrams and the cabin cruisers each seemed to have four crewmen. Those six vessels made up the body of the flotilla. They were mobile support fire. Looked as if the crew basically had side arms. The vessels showed machine gun emplacements on their bows and sterns. Openings on the sides of their hulls indicated rockets or torpedoes. Faster than Al could observe and analyze this information, the printer spit out the same and more detailed data. "Teddy, you stay inside the cabin." Al pulled Frenchie toward the door. "Don't come out in the line of fire under any circumstances. Do you hear me?"

"Yes, but."

"But, hell! We can't afford . . . the islands can't afford . . . to lose you!"

"But, it's you, not me, that's being t'reatened, me son."

"So, it's not you they're after." Al slammed the door shut behind him. "Not yet," he mumbled, leaving Teddy Morhead with no alternative but to believe that Al was dead serious about this. Al cleared his mind, reached inside himself and touched his Chi. He smiled and prepared himself for the potential of having to fight to his death in the defense of himself and his friend in the Pilot's cabin. Al picked his way to the bow of Remembrance; Frenchie, to the stern. The helm was being controlled by the Thai Chi Sea Defense program. Al hit the deck as M-60 fire strafed the bulletproof glass of the Pilot's cabin windows and ricocheted off the boat's armor-plated skin.

"At . . . ten . . . tion, crew of de Remembrance of T'ings Past. We don' wan' to harm you or your byoat. Surrender your weapons to the sea and fly a white pennant as a signal dat we can byoard you safely."

"Attention, crew of de Remembrance. You have t'irty seconds!"

All of a sudden a roar like a runaway locomotive flying down the tracks shattered the silence. Al knew that sound, and he knew what to expect. Seconds later one cruiser to the starboard of the trawler simply evaporated in a mushroom of exploding flame. "Jesus!" He gasped anyway. He looked down the deck toward where Frenchie Bryan slouched under a covering of coiled rope as if trying to stay out of sight.

When Frenchie saw Al grinning, he shot a thumb up as three more locomotive roars blew apart the other cruisers almost simultaneously. "Dem god'amned rocket launchers, Cap'n. I got such a deal, I just couldn't resist 'em!" he shouted above the exploding boats.

"I guess, at this moment, you fucking Frenchman, I'm damned glad you couldn't!"

M-60's erupted at both ends of Remembrance, bringing the remaining Betrams and Cigarettes under withering fields of fire in combination with the cannons at each side amidships. When the Cigarette roared in close as if trying to find an opening to board despite their resistance, Frenchie and Al unloaded with their assault rifles, killing at least three or four of the crewmen.

Before the stunned armada could even attempt to return effective fire, the Gattling mini-gun, which could cover a football field in one minute so completely that an ant wouldn't stand a very good chance of still being alive afterwards, opened up on the trawler itself. The computer homed its fire on the nerve center of the armada--a small communications center in the Pilot's cabin of the trawler.

As in Thai Chi, once the opponent has tipped his hand as to where he is going and what he is doing, then you simply beat him to it or used it against him. Within minutes, the Caribbean frothed with vessels sinking all around them. The trawler was listing at about seventy-five degrees and burning fiercely. But the computer defense system relentlessly continued to shoot at sinking targets and the crews abandoning ships all over the fiery, oil-slicked sea.

"Frenchie!"

"Cap'n?"

"Shut down that goddamned program, me-son . . . and quick! We can't just let it keep shooting people who are drowning and getting eaten by sharks."

"Aye, Cap'n!"

Al could hear Frenchie's footpads on the decking. He scanned the sea for survivors. Nothing moved in the oily, bloody churn but the sharks drawn by the vibrations of battle and the blood.

Frenchie shut down the computer as quickly as he could and immediately sent out a general distress call. In moments, the weapons ceased firing. A hurricane-eye silence fell over the sea.

"Hello. Anybody out dere? Dis be Chief Mate Frenchie Bryan of de yacht Remembrance of T 'ings Past out of St. Thomas, U.S. Virgin Islands. We have been attacked at sea. Many dead and wounded. Need help. Do you read me? Over?"

Frenchie's faced flushed all over . . . turning nearly purple. "Ah, yes sir, ah." Frenchie turned to Teddy. "Ah, Mr. Teddy, sir . . . ah. I mean . . . de Senate President be right here, sir." Frenchie shoved the headset toward Teddy Morhead as if it were some hot cassava. "It be de Governor, sir."

Teddy stepped closer and accepted the headset, placing it on his large head. "Ted Morhead here. Over.

"Yes, Esteban. Yes, Esteban. We know about it first hand, believe me, me-son!" Teddy almost had to laugh. "Yes, we just fought off an attack by a small armada. As soon as we can return we must meet. You remember the agreed upon emergency meeting place and how to calculate the time we should meet there?" He paused while waiting for the Governor's reply. "Good. See you then. Over and out."

Teddy turned to Al who had just walked through the doorway, a blank look on his face and in his eyes. "Esteban has received a threatening note too."

"Dat sure 'nough means you be next Mr. Teddy, sir!" Frenchie blurted out before he could cover his big mouth with his knurled hands.

"Just what our guest needs to hear right now, Mister Bryan!"

"It's okay." Teddy punched Frenchie playfully with a softball size fist and winked. "Hell, I always was one to feel slighted if I wasn't on the all-star team, me-son."

* * * * *

They only fished two survivors out of the bloodstained churned up sea. The battle with the growing shark population got the rest. One of the two captives had his leg chewed off at the knee while they were hauling him in.

Al quickly tied a tourniquet above the mangled left knee cap and sealed off the wound as best he could with sterile bandages Frenchie kept in the Pilot's cabin medicine chest and a rain slicker. Al thought about how lucky he and Teddy had been that there was no blood in the water when those sharks came after them.

Two hours later as Al loosed the tourniquet, he finally tried to question the man. The victim seemed not to be in such deep shock as earlier. "How do you feel?" Jesus, Al thought. What a thing to ask a guy who just got his leg chewed off by a shark. "Ah . . . why were you attacking my boat?"

The man's skin was the color of tannic acid stained water in mangrove swamps. He stared through Al's eyes, seemingly without even seeing Al. Al resisted the compulsion to grab the guy's raw stump and gouge the open wound. That would sure as hell make the motherfucker talk. In Nam, he probably would've done it. But. "Why did you attack my boat?"

The other prisoner was a female. She was "dark, dark, dark" as Frenchie put it. "I am a prisoner of war in a holy revolution against de American Imperialist pigs!" I will not answer any questions or give you any information. I am protected under the Geneva Convention."

"Horse shit, honey!" Al hurled back at the woman with a trace of a Patois in her dialect . . . Dominican Patois, not Haitian, he thought. He had taken a strong interest in dialects after he read *Huckleberry Finn* for the first time. "Your kind isn't protected by the Geneva or any other Convention . . . no way!" Samuel Clemens claimed to have used, and probably did use, as many as twenty or more dialects in that one book. Today, they are rare in the states . . . dialects, that is, not books. Television, in the wake of the second wave (the tidal wave of industrialization), had just about reduced everyone to sounding like Tom Brokaw on the NBC Nightly News.

The Caribbean, fortunately, was a cornucopia of dialects, from the Dutch-based Papiamento to Patois and English-and-Spanish-based Creole or calypso. And each island has its own unique accent. Sometimes more than one accent or dialect was spoken on the same island . . . like Dominica where Patois and English-based calypso or Creole are spoken.

The woman threw a look at Al that was somewhere between a snarl and a licentious smile. "Well, I guess you be right. I mean, mon, you could just take me right here and now and dere'd be not a t'ing I could do 'bou'tit . . . right?" She twisted against the bonds that held her arms up and back from her waist. Her wrists were tied to the bulkhead of the Pilot's cabin.

37

As she stretched against the ropes that held her, the Velcro strips down the front of her camouflage shirt pulled apart revealing sculptured and polished ebony breasts, glistening with sweat. "Right?"

Her brown-pink tongue curled from between the bright even teeth of a model, which filled her mouth between her thick dark lips, which she caressed with her tongue. Al could feel his loins swelling in spite of the situation.

"Touch my nipples, Al-fred Crist. Feel how hard dey be, aching for your fingers," she groaned, "and your hot wet tongue. Come on, mon, and find out what you be missin'."

In other times, in other iterations, he knew that he might have done it, reached out and tasted the delights of fucking the enemy. He'd done it more than once before. This was an invitation to the inside, to find out what the fuck was going on. But, how did she know his name? How did she know his name?

CHAPTER 4

A LITTLE CARIBBEAN OBEAH

Limbo Leonard held his toothpick body parallel to the floor, just three inches above the cement. His head bent back toward the audience on the patio at East End Bay Resort's breeze-swept beachside dining room and dance floor as his body swayed to a calypso by Iree and the Gumbies. His mouth spewed flames at the star-salted sky like another of the flaming torches surrounding the patio. Fronds thick on coconut palms rattled against each other in the "Trades" blowing up from the Sahara.

The resort was the only place on the island you could count on for a good old fashioned West Indian tourist show under the stars, surrounded by palms and sea grape trees pushing against the white sand beach towards the sea. Limbo dancers spitting fire, mocko jumbies dancing on tall stilts, and steel bands beating out melodious calypso favorites like "Marianne" and "The Banana Boat Song" satiated the sunburned and rum-soaked tourists with that Caribbean feeling, then, sent them back to their condos and hotel rooms to sleep off the sunburn and the planters punch.

They marched in the Carnival parade each year and played in clubs and restaurants during season. Iree Gumbs also worked with Al as an investigator when he needed one, and Al worked with the band when they'd let him. Mostly he wrote songs with Iree, but sometimes, after everyone had left, Iree Gumbs, Al Crist, and the band jammed raggae until the wee hours.

Tonight, though, Al needed to relax. It had been a rough day, and it might not be over yet. He still had to meet the mysterious Eloise Anselm-Smith, Publisher of *Mystique* and courier for Doc Streeter. He recalled Doc speaking of her often, especially a few years back when she went through a pretty bad divorce and came out of it by starting the magazine. He had to give her credit. Anyone who could come out of a bad situation with a quality book like *Mystique* had to be good. And, she had the good taste to use his pieces.

Across the room, a typical island "come on" seemed to be in process. A young hulk of a taxi driver Al had seen around. Mr. Slick you might call him. He was everywhere in the islands, lurking at the bars where tourists are known to go, cruising the narrow island roads scouring the place for damsels in distress of one sort or another. After all, women did seem to be attracted to St. Thomas by some vague notion of getting screwed by some natural island man. So, the cockiness with which these Mr. Slicks approached their chosen passtimes--which for many was more of a profession--of preying on tourist women was not unwarranted. You certainly couldn't fault Mr. Slick for his choice of women. The lady he was "coming on" to was striking in every way. Her raven hair and black pools of eyes accentuated her sunburned skin. Even from a distance her presence excited him. He could imagine how she must be affecting the taxi driver who was so close to her.

Mr. Slick put his hand on the woman's shoulder and leaned forward. Al was out of his seat before anyone could have noticed. He instinctively felt protective toward her even from eight tables away. He held his space, his head feeling like it was suspended by a thread from the eaves of the roof above him, his knees slightly flexed. The weight of his body swayed from one side to the other imperceptibly so that he was not, at any given moment, double-weighted. Waiting . . .

The taxi driver's lips were merely centimeters from the young raven hair's own sweet plump lips when she exploded from her chair in one clean motion as if she were propelled by some force. Al was to learn later that force was her legs! It was when Al saw her move like that that he knew it was Mr. Slick who was in trouble, not the raven-haired beauty. For at the same time that she exploded she also exploded in silence. She grasped Mr. Slick's pressure point at the intersect of his neck and left shoulder between her left thumb and forefinger without even the frightened taxi driver realizing what was happening. The young tigress was subtle in her movements. No one else in the restaurant seemed to be aware of what just happened. All eyes in that restaurant were still glued to Limbo Leonard swaying under the limbo pole, fire spewing from his mouth to the beat of calypso rhythms beaten out on the steel pans. The taxi driver was paralyzed.

Al relaxed, sat down again as he watched that extraordinary woman let the driver go immediately after establishing herself as if he were some cowering little wimp, giving him a mild shove and a killing stare from her black eyes. Mr. Slick remained paralyzed for another moment, then slouched off towards the beat of the steel drums as the fire-eating Leonard made it under the limbo pole at three inches. The crowd cheered. The young woman reseated herself between her two female companions. Her exposed arms, upper back and chest above her breasts rippled as she smoothed her soot black dress as if she had just brushed away a less-than-bothersome mosquito.

International journalist or not, Alfred Crist suffered from shyness. He didn't have trouble with the Governor of the Virgin Islands or a CARICOM Prime Minister or even the President. But, woman? That was another story entirely. She confounded him, confused him. She tied his otherwise relatively glib and sometimes even entertaining tongue into a jumble of gift-wrap bows. He was at her mercy! Yet, he was astounded into action.

"Georges?" Al flagged down the Maitre d'. He had known Georges since he first moved into the villa on the east end of St. Thomas. It seemed that Georges had been the Maitre d' at the East End Resort Restaurant since anyone could remember.

"Monsieur, Alfred?" Georges stopped primly at the table tucking his white towel over his right arm and bowing a little stiffly. He nodded his silver-and-red hair toward one of his all-time favorite customers. Monsieur Alfred had taste. He was a pleasure to serve... always.

"Georges, my good man," Al kidded. "How many times over the past three years have I steered, or personally brought, to you major parties which spent major dollars...beau coup francs...oui? --and provided you and your staff with lavish tips...no?"

"Oh, Monsieur Alfred, more zhan I could ever count, I assure you!" Georges grinned from gray-and-red sideburn to gray-and-red sideburn. He knew that here was a man after his own heart. Monsieur Alfred wanted something tonight in return for some of those other times and the times still to come when he helped old Georges. "What may I do for you specially tonight, Monsieur Alfred, mon ami? I am totally at your disposal...."

"You see the young woman at that table over there across the room," Al asked trying not to point at the table where the raven-haired youth laughed and talked with her friends who were just as attractive, if not more so, than she was on the surface. But there was something more.

"Zhe young woman in the low cut soot black gown? With zhe two charming companions?" Georges responded without ever taking his eyes off Al's face. "She's wearing a crepe gown, I believe, monsieur."

"You never cease to amaze me, Georges." Al shook his head. "How did you know who?"

"Simply a matter of deduction, monsieur. You have always displayed excellent taste in your food, your wines...and your women."

"Thank you, Georges," Al smiled.

"Zhat young woman is zhe only vintage lady I've seen in here tonight or for many a night." Georges smiled broadly and blew a bow by Al like he had never seen in any restaurant in St. Thomas. Al applauded softly in admiration. "Bravo, Georges . . . bravo!"

"Merci, Monsieur Alfred. Merci."

"I would like very much to meet her, Georges. But you know me all these years. I'm not the most aggressive."

Georges' ever-broadening smile erupted into an effusiveness not normally like him. He reserved this kind of pure pleasure for very special situations and he knew in that moment that this was to be one of those very special moments, one he was being asked to play a substantial role in . . . Cupid or Pander . . . take your pick of types. He was going to be able to put this brilliant and loveable young man he had known and come to admire and respect over the past several years together with that exquisite young woman at table twenty-four. Every person in the entire restaurant, including Limbo Leonard, had noticed her at one point in the evening or another. Yet no one but Monsieur Alfred had noticed her with the drunken taxi driver called Sabo. Sabo was, as might be expected, a continuing source of embarrassment. If he were not the brother-in-law of the hotel manager, he would have been banned from the restaurant and hotel long ago. Monsieur Alfred had conducted himself like the gentleman he was...of course. "It will give me zhe greatest pleasure to assist you, Monsieur Alfred, in your romantic quest. We Frenchmen appreciate such matters in a very special way, as you know?"

Al nodded his head. "Yes. I was hoping you'd say something like that."

* * * * *

"Jesus!" was all Al could muster when old Georges bounded out of the kitchen with a baked Alaska and a bottle of Courvoisier cognac Napoleon.

"Mademoiselles.... Compliments of Monsieur Alfred Crist, zhe world famous journalist who lives here with us at zhe East End Bay Resort...." Georges' glance in Al's direction seemed almost like a full bow with trumpets as he produced from behind him a clear, cut-crystal vase containing one long-stemmed American Beauty rose.

Ruby red like the young woman's lips and the flush that flamed at her cheeks as Georges presented the rose to her and she in turn bent her eyes, almost bashfully it seemed, in his direction.

"Alfred Crist, you say?"

"Oui, mademoiselle."

"Please ask this world-famous journalist to come over and share some of this wonderful desert and cognac so that we won't all get fat and drunk separately." She giggled behind a delicate hand that held firm the rose in the cut-crystal vase. "And, tell him . . . tell him that I have something for him."

Al couldn't, for the life of him, figure out how in the hell Georges could have come up with an American Beauty rose--a fresh one at that! --At ten-thirty at night in St. Thomas between the ocean and the sea. But there it was!

A little obeah on a balmy Caribbean night.

* * * * *

"Eloise Anselm-Smith, Mr. Crist."

"Oh, no!" He felt the blood rushing through his neck. "Really?"

"Really. I guess you don't answer your messages?"

"No . . . ah . . . Ms. Anselm-Smith. That's not the case at all. Ah . . . I." He turned to the other two women seated at the table and gestured with his arms. "Help me here, ladies. I'm a man in distress." They chuckled and shrugged their bleached but burned shoulders. "You need to do something about those shoulders, ladies. Aloe Vera. Take a warm shower to open up the pores and then apply aloe vera liberally. It will keep you from blistering and preserve the tan."

43

"Thank you, Mr. Crist." She was a petite redhead with a mid-western non-accented voice. "My name is Trudy Jerrigan. I'm from Tulsa." She paused and turned to her left to her tall, slender companion. "And this is Gina de Loca from the Bronx."

"Welcome to paradise, Trudy . . . Gina." Al turned back to Lois. "Lois."

"Hurumph."

"Listen, I can explain. I ran into some very unexpected and unpleasant characters today. Well, anyway. I did call. I left a message for you at your hotel that I would be here until midnight. You see I sometimes jam with the band."

"Oh, really?"

"I detect a taint of sarcasm or is it disbelief in your voice, do I not?"

"You do."

"Very well, when the band breaks, I'll get my friend and co-worker Iree Gumbs over here to straighten this all out. After all, it's bad enough that you think I don't return messages from beautiful and brave women, but it's even worse if you think that I would lie to you."

"Well, anyway. Here's the envelope from Doc. He said it was confidential and very important. Otherwise, I certainly wouldn't have been playing telephone tag with you. I don't make a habit of chasing after men."

"I'm sure you'd never have need to do that, Lois." Al's lips trembled in a nervous smile as he accepted the manila envelop from Lois. He tore open the sealed flap and pulled out a single sheet of plain typewriter paper. Typed on the sheet was a short note:

> Yes. Just like you suspected,
> V.P. planning Carnival Coup
> D'etat. U.S. wants excuse to
> bathe in the Caribbean Basin.
> Watch your ass! And Lois's!
>
>
> Doc

"Now," Al muttered as he folded the piece of paper into eighths with the typing inside so that it was not visible to anyone else at the table and tore the sheet into small pieces along the creases. "He believes me."

"What?"

"Oh, nothing, Lois . . . nothing. Does anyone have a light?"

Trudy pulled a butane lighter from her purse. "Here, Al."

"Thanks, Trudy." He dropped the pieces of the note into the ashtray, lighting the final shred and dropping it onto the small pile. He shrugged as they all stared at him. "I always do that with my mail after I've read it. Don't you?" He laughed.

They laughed.

"Georges?"

"Yes, monsieur Al?"

"More cognac, if you please."

* * * * *

Al's body broke out of the crystal water less than a foot from shore. White moon light captured in drops of sea water cascaded over his body as he emerged from the black-and-moon-lit Caribbean Sea like Poseidon, the half-empty bottle of Couvosier Napolean like a jade trident in his hand as he raised it up towards Lois like an offering, startling her out of a sexual reverie which had sort of flowed from the moon, borne by the balmy breezes off of the sea, to the warmth of her loins.

Al's lean brown body splashed ashore, a silhouette in the moonlight. Cokies croaked in a hesitant calypso harmony infusing the night air like moisture. The sea dribbled down his chest and taut abdominal muscles into the dark blue patch of spandex by Eminence that barely covered his crotch. Lois licked her red lips. She could feel her tongue in every fiber of her being as she rolled it across her now moist lips thinking, feeling not her tongue but the beauty he held inside that dark blue spandex bikini. Lois glanced around her.

45

The beach was cloistered by clusters of mahogany, coconut palms and sea grape trees as well as high thick lemon grass. No one at all on the beach. It was as if they were the only two people in this entire tropical paradise. That's why he had suggested that they come here after the club closed. She was sure of that.

As Al approached her, she dropped the straps of her beige bikini top so that they fell forward in front of her pulling what little material there was further away from her breasts. She shuddered.

Al stopped dead in his tracks.

Lois could no longer control herself, nor did she want to. She was sure that all of a sudden five Grey Line Tour groups could show up and she wouldn't change her plan of attack. She glided up onto her knees, her bikini top no longer covering her left breast at all. Her lips, full and soft as the rose petals on the American Beauty Al had given her the night before, were flung recklessly open exposing her teeth just parted and a tongue which reached out from between those gleaming teeth.

* * * * *

Lois lost her breath as she recalled last night with Mr. Alfred Crist, world famous journalist (who obviously had the Maitre d' on his side), the most exciting man she had ever met, but he didn't seem to realize how exciting a man he was at all, which somewhat surprised her.

She rolled over to nibble Al's ear and snuggle. No Al. "Al?"

"Got to get moving, babe."

His voice came from the shadows of the dressing end of his bedroom suite. Lois thought she could see him bent over tying his Nikes but she wasn't sure in the darkness. "You haven't even told me what that damned note from Doc was all about . . . and after I brought it all the way from the States for you."

"Well . . . when I get back, babe . . . after my exercises and my run. Okay?"

Lois shrugged. What was she to say? It wasn't okay. That in the less than twelve hours they'd known each other, she felt that she somehow had a right to know. That, already, this stinking surrogate "brother" of hers was the only man in the world, including "daddy" Doc, who could call her "babe" and get away with it. "Okay." He was already gone, into the front hallway moving toward the great room. The digital clock glowed: 5:17.

Lois felt that she already knew Al pretty well, even though they had only known each other since last night. He seemed to be the kind of person that you either got to know very well very quickly or not very well ever. She knew, for example, that he would run extra hard this morning . . . probably even extra distance because he would feel badly about having breached routine . . . no matter how much he enjoyed what they did. And she also knew him well enough to know that he always enjoyed sex . . . with her or with any other woman who desired him . . . and there were lots of them. She was sure of that. Her impression of Alfred Crist was that he was something special. He was the single most sensitive man she had ever known. Uninhibited in sex but bashful in bars. Nearly twice her age yet he seemingly had twice her stamina.

"Damn the man!" she chuckled. He was more dedicated and regimented now at forty-seven than she was ten years ago at seventeen when she decided that body building was what she wanted to go for in life. Those ten years were like ten greased rungs on a ladder, but she'd known it would be tough. She had been prepared for that. What she hadn't really been prepared for adequately was success, stardom if you will, in the field of woman's body building and in modeling.

Her thirty assorted international and national titles established the more model-like musculature as the sport's standard. And her image as a thinking, "hot" young woman of the times who attended Radcliffe on scholarship doomed the stereotype of the female jock to a deserving extinction.

Through all of this she felt like she was in a continual state of drowning and it was five years and two national titles before Lois got herself onto the right track financially. Then she got married, and there was no more right financial track, no more career.

But, she loved starting new operations, either out of thin air or from the wreckage of a dying or dead one. So, she tried to apply her passion for new endeavors to her marriage. When their relationship continued to deteriorate despite her efforts, the challenge of building something anew or out of the ruin of divorce suddenly became quite important to Lois. It substituted, in

47

many ways, for the struggle she had made a part of her life to be the best female body builder in the world and then the best wife in the world.

She seemed to have been considerably more successful in sport than in marriage. Lois pulled her fingers through the tangles in her long raven hair and stretched against the cool sheets. "Yes, sir. If I had Al's dedication, I could be world champion again," she cooed. "But who wants to be world champion again? Well, maybe world champion in the areas of the Two B's: business and bedroom." Lois pulled the breeze-cooled sheets up over her.

The clock read: 5:30

* * * * *

The left side of his body jarred as his waffle-soled Nike hit the pavement. His breath was measured. In. Two. Three. Four. Right shoe hit. Out. Two. Three. Four. Left shoe hit. Smells of things growing and the same things decaying engulfed him as did the high lemon grass and thickets of bushes and mahogany trees clutching at the edges of both sides of the narrow, cracked black top road.

Alfred Crist had grown up with the same idea as most of us about adventures in some paradise or another . . . something out of Melville or Boroughs or on television staring Gardner Mckay as Adam Troy captain of the schooner Tiki. He sailed from port to exotic port in the Pacific. That had been in the fifties. Television was new. Paradise had not yet been lost, John Milton's protestations to the contrary. That was before Ferlinghetti and Basho had entered his life . . . before Wayne Morse had enthused him and Madame Nhu had incensed him . . . before Vietnam . . . before Moses Promised Land Gumbs became a missing in action statistic on his way up Monkey Mountain. He ascended into . . ..

He knew that his idea of adventures in paradise today certainly differed from that one embedded in his past. Stimulating work was important to his paradise today in a way that it never was, or could have been, to Captain Adam Troy of the schooner Tiki. That necessitated conveniences he would never have tolerated such as a sixty-foot motor yacht with an onboard computer and a modem to his home base computer in St. Thomas. If he had to have stimulating work, then he had to be able to cover and communicate the assignments efficiently. That could be done a lot easier

48

from Remembrance of Things Past than from things past like the Tiki. To cover the Caribbean for the most important news organizations in the world meant to be computerized and plugged in.

His paradise also required social and political involvement--anathema to the Adam Troy's both then and now. Yes, Al Crist's paradise was truly another kind of paradise altogether from the one where the Tiki would forever plow the waves of the emerald Pacific in search of adventure in a vacuum.

Perfect Virgin Islands mornings like this one made him realize that this new kind of paradise with its computers and diesel inboards wasn't all that bad after all, even with the cloud of the attack yesterday and the growing assassination plot lurking behind the crest of every hill he ran like a car or truck or safari bus waiting to side-swipe the runner. There were several hills and blind curves in this stretch of his morning run between his villa and Red Hook at the eastern tip of St. Thomas where it seemed that cars and trucks really did lie in wait for runners coming around a curve or over the crest of a hill. Ah, what price paradise?

A brown pelican tucked its wings and plummeted toward the pink-as-coral water of the marina bay as Al picked up his pace for the last half-mile of his four mile run. The last half-mile wound its way along the marina road onto the beach. Usually he ran three on weekdays, four to six on weekends. "The brown pelican has poor eyesight," Al remembered reading somewhere. "Yet it must rely on its eyesight to fish. Therefore it lives only in areas where the sea waters are clear enough for the pelican to actually see the fish it dives for."

Teddy had asked him last night on the way back to port what he thought about the situation in ethical terms. He actually asked, "Who has truth and right on their side, Al? Us? Or the frigging VILA group?" He asked as if somebody really did. "You know them better than me?

"We don't know if those two in the cabin are VILA? We don't know yet."

"Then let's go down there," Teddy pointed below decks to where the captives were stowed, "and question them again until we get answers!"

The brown pelican hit the water like an anchor but bobbed up onto the surface like a buoy, throwing its beak up and back several times to store its catch before taking off for more sunrise fishing. That was the only truth and right he knew. Dawn and pelicans fishing and running on the beach. That's what he'd told Teddy too. Yet, he knew he was lying, covering up what he believed to really be the truth that he had uncovered in his investigations into U.S. activities in the Caribbean over the past couple of years . . . that the Vice President of the United States was planning and supporting a coup in the Virgin Islands so the U.S. could gain a renewed military presence in the Caribbean. Now, Doc's note had verified his worst fears. Somehow, he knew that he wouldn't be able to simply avoid this new kind of truth that was emerging.

The sun inched its way above the soft green peaks of Tortola into the usual bank of clouds that were pushed across these islands by the trade winds from Africa. A lot more than simple slavery connected these islands to Africa. There were times when Al was sure he could hear the bodies of men and women who leaped as slaves from Lovers' Leap during the otherwise bloodless St. John rebellion and fell to their deaths as free men and women, splashing like huge pelicans into the see-through sea. It was the first known organized slave rebellion in the western world, long before Nat Turner or Harper's Ferry.

This part of the morning run was his favorite, when he was finally really loose and really sweating. He picked it up and stretched it out to the max along the pounded coral sand of the quarter-mile beach strip running in front of East End Bay Villas. As he tried to explain his life to people, to colleagues in particular, he would stammer for words then sputter out "I mean, it's right out of the frigging movies!" The power of his body that he'd held in reserve surged forward as he sprinted for home, bone-white sand spitting out behind his flying Nikes.

As Al pulled up, jogging in place, the pelican, like Icarus, soared into the sun now blazing out just above the cloud bank in time for his cool downs--that final ritual of stretching out the muscles and tendons after completing his run. Ritual was essential. T.S. Elliot had, by the time he was Al's age, joined the Anglican church just so he could get some ritual back into his life. That, for the moment, seemed to be another truth. All of a sudden, the morning was becoming cluttered with truths.

He began to stretch out his Achilles tendons, hamstrings, and lower back with the yoga stretch called the cow. He bent from the waist with his chin tucked into his chest grasping his ankles with his fingers and pulled his body to his legs until his forehead touched his shins. He held for a count of twenty, released and came upright slowly.

Next he did leg stretches with his left heel first, then his right heel, propped on a wooden trellis almost hidden among the sea grape trees. He bent forward from the waist until his lips kissed his shin as far toward the ankle as he could reach and held for a count of fifteen before releasing and raising upright so he could switch from left leg to right.

"But wait!" he muttered in his mind as he began his lunges. Maybe ritual is the same truth as the brown pelicans fishing at dawn. Isn't that, after all, simply a particular form of ritual?

After completing his lunges, Al entered an opening in the dense sea grape stand on the beach. Surely, he thought, this was his church. These were some of his ceremonies, his rituals. The growth of trees was controlled by treated wooden trellis supports. These supports created a tunnel amidst the sea grape trees. An oversized towel awaited him as it did every morning, left by his housekeeper, Herbert, each evening before she left work. He toweled off as he ambled through the tunnel of sea grape branches and leaves and lattice work to the back entrance of his villa. It took awhile to get used to his housekeeper having a man's name. She had explained it to him once. How her father had planned to name the firstborn in his family after his father, Herbert. Then she was born instead of a boy. So, she got the name instead.

Out of the sea grape trees, a dark shadow flashed across the corner of Al's eye. He sensed that he was about to take a blow designed to at least cripple or maim him. And, he knew he could not totally prevent that first blow from landing. He leaned in the opposite direction from the shadow's anticipated blow and concentrated on transforming the pain from the blow's impact toward outward force through his late block and counterblow and kick. He became the pain. He felt the jaw of the shadow shatter under the heel of his foot.

* * * * *

Al was sure he must've blacked out from the impact and pain of the blows from the shadow's obviously well schooled fists. When he became aware again, his shadowy assailant was nowhere to be seen. Lois trembled at his side near the back door of the villa. "You wouldn't tell me what was wrong when I gave you that note from Doc. You just burned the damned note!" She stamped her bare feet. "And now you've just about been killed by an assassin right here in front of my own eyes.

"I demand to know, damn it! Why?" She sniffled, struggled with the tears that wanted to flow freely. Finally, she began to bawl. "I . . . you . . . I . . . I . . . damnit! . . . have . . . a . . . right to . . . to know." She lowered her eyes towards Al. "Look at you down there. My own personal guide to paradise . . . knocked flat on his ass by some invisible assailant. Don't I have a right to know why?"

"Yes." Al pushed upward, almost sitting. "I guess. It sure seems like you do at that." He waved towards the doorway. "My deck pants in the kitchen." She was nearly through the door before he could finish his instructions. "Right rear pocket. There's a note."

Jesus his ribs hurt when he moved. The bastards didn't waste any time. Wonder how they found out so fast about what old Remembrance did to their little armada?

"I thought you burned all of your mail after you'd read it?" Lois tried to joke as she stumbled over the threshold from the kitchen to the back of the villa, holding a crumpled piece of gray paper between her hands and trying to read the message in red letters.

ALFRED CRIST:
YOU WERE ONCE A COMRADE. WE NEED YOUR
HELP NOW. YOU ARE EITHER FOR US OR AGAINST US!

RAS UJAMMA I

Lois's fingers trembled around the gray paper. "What is this? As she spoke she seemed to be trying to get rid of the scrap of paper as if it were some disease.

"It was delivered to my P.O. Box yesterday morning. I didn't take it all that seriously, you know. Hell, I've been subject to threats and even attacks over the years when I've gotten too close to somebody or something. But, just to be on the safe side, Frenchie and I decided to push up the fishing trip we'd been planning to test this new spear gun Frenchie invented . . . really, an excuse to get my friend Teddy Morhead, the Senate President, away from the rat race and maybe give us some lead time to think things out . . . and time to brief Teddy on all I know about VILA. Baby, we had to move fast and secret. No one could know. That's why you couldn't get through

52

to me. Usually, I would've had a shore to ship transfer set up. But I didn't want anyone getting to us.

"Then, last night. The phone call at the club while we were jamming? That was Teddy. He had a similar note in his P.O. Box when we returned from our trip. Only his threatened him with death if he did not step down by Carnival Parade day."

"And Doc's note?"

"He confirmed something I've suspected for a long time."

"What?"

"The V.P. is behind this. It's a plot to give the U.S. a reason to send troops into the Caribbean."

Lois stared at the crumpled note. "So that's why I couldn't get you on the phone?" She pouted and kissed him softly on the lips. "And all the time I thought you were just blowing me off."

"No way. It took an attack at sea to keep me from returning your call. I mean it was an armada that hit us, babe! Eight cabin cruiser types, four cigarettes, and a trawler. Goddamn! I think they were just out to capture me. I don't think they even knew that Teddy was onboard.

"It was Frenchie's weapons system that saved our asses. It just obliterated them before they could even get to us. We did take two prisoners from the sea, however." His voice seemed to lodge in his throat just for a moment. "Ah . . . we rescued them from the wreckage of the trawler."

"Then, where the hell are they? Maybe they know something about all this?"

Al's memory flashed to Remembrance later the previous night. He and Teddy had returned below decks to question them one more time . . . to finally get some damned answers about the attack. They found the two prisoners dead in the cabin. The smallish man with the chewed off leg had his head split open by a karate star with a red and black yin yang painted on both sides.

The woman no longer resisted against her restraints. Al had released her arms earlier. But she now lay in a pool of her own blood. With a karate star sill vice-gripped between her hands, she had ripped open her abdomen allowing her Chi to escape from her body.

"They didn't survive the night." He stood, held onto Lois's shoulder for a moment, then stumbled into the kitchen. He fumbled through his trouser pockets until he found what he was looking for. "Lois! Come here, baby!" As she passed the kitchen thresh hold, he held the karate stars towards her. "They killed themselves with these."

"This is not what I had in mind when I decided to take three months off in paradise, Al." She wagged her head, tears smearing her flushed cheeks. "Not one little bit."

* * * * *

It was time for the satellite communications link to open up for messages at the office of the Department of the Interior. "I've got to get onto my computer, baby . . . report this shit to my buddy, Santurce." He shook his head. It was clearing a little now but not fast enough for him. As he tried to walk toward his study, his legs seemed to remain unconvinced that his head was clearing. They wobbled and buckled. He still needed Lois's support as he opened the study door. The odor of rosewood inlaid in the door acted like smelling salts, snapping his olfactory nerves alive and thus his head. The rest of his body followed quickly.

"Okay, now?"

"Yeah."

Lois stepped back from him as he entered the doorway on his own steam, then closed the rosewood inlaid door behind him and locked it, sealing himself inside his inner-sanctum of West Indian woods, computers and works by everyone from the Caribbean poet and playwright Derek Walcott to William Butler Yeats, from West Indies scholar and historian Isaac Dookan to Arnold Toynbee. "These sweet shelves," he mumbled as he slowly worked his way across the highly polished island stone floor toward his computer workstation on the far side of the library. It covered about the same floor space of a small house . . . somewhere around eleven hundred square feet. The walls towered to a cathedral ceiling with stained glass skylights overhead. The walls were slats of polished teak, mahogany, and a mixture of other West Indian woods, which created a mosaic of colors and grains throughout the room. The island stone floor was ground flat and smooth as the surface of a Main Street jewel and polished with oils and polymers to create a nearly impregnable surface that glistened in the morning sunlight filtering down through the skylights and the eastern bank of windows above the computer station. So, by design, he and his computer and bank of four screens were bathed in soft direct sunlight most of the day.

This was not a library like so many others, dead or dying. It was vibrant with Al's tools, his research, his work. Aside from the basic library books on the floor-to-ceiling shelves, all of his personal writing materials and primitive research items such as books, ledgers, articles, notes, and papers were stored in deep cedar bins along one side. They were considerably fewer now than they had been. He employed a couple of local high school students from All Saints Anglican School to sort of OJT with him on the computers by in-putting all of his personal materials onto diskettes for storage. Once that was completed, Al placed the original manuscripts in a bank vault in St. Kitts. Both of the students were in the running for Presidential Scholar. He was very proud of them. He was also proud of his computer system, one that could call up information from the middle of the Panama Canal if necessary while he was on Remembrance.

"You and this Santurce are real close, huh?"

"I guess you could say that."

Lois's voice continued to chatter at him through the rosewood-inlaid door as if he were standing right in front of her instead of the door. Al could picture her dark body glistening still in the morning sunlight as it streamed through the skylights in the hallway while she spoke.

"I mean, the only time Juan Santurce's ever even graced these islands with his presence was because of a direct--and I might add beautifully engineered--invitation from you that he come down and spend a week with you on Remembrance."

Al sat down in front of his terminal workstation and booted up the system. "Yeah, and I got the governor and the senate president out on my yacht for dinner one evening, an overnight stay and a sunrise cruise the next morning. Now that kind of shit's hard for anybody to resist."

55

"Yeah," she sighed. "I can imagine." She paused seeming to picture a night with Al at the helm. "So I hear it, the whole basis of the great relations the islands now enjoy with the U.S. comes from that outing on Remembrance. What was it? Two years ago?"

Al logged in and typed the code for his patch with Santurce's office. He dialed the top-secret line telephone number. The modem dialed and engaged the computer at the receiving end. "Almost three years by now. Right after Teddy was elected and made Senate President as a freshman senator. I'm still not sure if I would've called in such a favor from my friend Santurce if my good friend Teddy hadn't been elected as the leader of the Senate. Most of those other clowns who called themselves senators wouldn't get much help from me. That's for goddamned sure!"

"What kind of favor?

"Well." Al hesitated. "You see, Juan and I knew each other in the Nam. Sort of hush-hush stuff, you know. Once, on Monkey Mountain, I was in a position to save my ass or make him look good. I did both! He always felt he owed me. I didn't. I subscribe more to the notion that if you save someone's life then they are, in a sense, your responsibility. After all, they wouldn't be around if not for your saving them. By now both of us are so into the other, nobody could possibly keep count."

"Oh, I see. So that's why he came down here even though the pressure was strongly against him coming?"

Monitor one flashed confirmation of the code he had entered. The patch was cleared to Washington. "Amazing though."

"What's amazing?"

"The whole time thing. It's been nearly three years now since the Governor, the Senate President, and the Assistant Secretary of the Interior for International Affairs issued a joint communiqué entitled the 'Remembrance Communiqué.' It was really a memorandum of understanding between the Virgin Islands and the U.S. government. The first such document other than the basic Organic Acts which govern the islands. Yet, it seems like just last week or last month since it all happened. And, I guess, the V.P. wasn't, and still isn't, very happy about it all."

"<<<ACCESS NOW>>>TOP SECRET SECURITY LEVEL<<<TOP SECRET PATH>>>"

The computers were getting edgy. "Well, after that story how about some breakfast?"

"Shit, I thought I was breakfast!"

Al laughed as he typed in his security code and began his message.

ENTER. TOP SECRET. FOR SANTURCE EYES ONLY.

<<<SCRAMBLE>>>

Just the way I like to eat my eggs and send my messages of possible coup d'etat to Juan Santurce sculptor turned bureaucrat whom he had known intimately as one artist to another who each had to turn to other means of making a living over the years. They had been friends since Vietnam when he was a field team leader for military intelligence operations and Al was a military intelligence operative sleeping as a squad leader buck sergeant in the Big Red One. Juan Santurce was his contact then. He was Al's most valued political contact in D.C. now. Just like in the Nam, Santurce'd get them help quick. Hopefully before they finished breakfast.

CHAPTER 5

PROMISED LAND'S LITTLE BROTHER

Al felt like he was walking point, even though he was only driving his open-top jeep along Mafolie Road towards Drake Seat. That was where Iree had said to pick him up. The fact that this thin winding road with its blind curves and steep hills was strangled with dense growths of Tamarind--narrow brown pods dangling like giant fingers from their branches--, mango and breadfruit trees, and the ever-present lemon grass seemed to make it more like a jungle path than a civilized roadway. He had never liked walking point. He didn't like the feeling one little bit, either. It made him nervous.

But he still remembered well Promised Land Gumbs walking point. They called him Promised Land partly because he walked point more than anyone else in the squad and was still alive. He was better at it than any of them. And, strange as it might seem, he never seemed to be nervous about it. Sometimes he even acted as though he enjoyed it. Also, partly because his given name was Moses. That added significantly to the importance attached to this point man's (and Al's best friend in the Monkey Mountain forests) nickname. Most important was the fact that he was from the U.S. Virgin Islands--the American Paradise. It sounded like a promised land to them when he'd talk about his islands at night around the fire if they were allowed to have one or in the suffocating darkness of the jungles and forests if they weren't. He spun yarns about night fishing off the reefs in a lantern-lit dingy with drop lines and cruising the white sand beaches by day. He described how the bikini's barely covered the tanning flesh of young secretaries from Des Moines or New York who'd saved all year to come down during the cheaper summer months and have a tropical island romance or the super rich spoiled daughters of cattle farmers, oilmen, or stock brokers who were also looking for a little tropical island romance but usually during "season."

Whitman the Poet trailed what was left of the squad. He humped a BAR. Al liked the hell out of having the instant field of fire that came with a Browning Automatic Rifle and someone who really knew how to use it covering his squad's ass. And with Poet it was damned well covered too. He could pen a haiku on a VC's chest with that BAR of his at fifty meters.

That left Stinky Fairchild humping the radio in the middle of the pack, never far from Al's side. Then Al and, of course, Errol Flynn Brown. E.F., as they all called him, looked exactly like Errol Flynn during the height of his swashbuckling days...only E.F. was a black man. It was a combination that made him virtually a god to girls of every persuasion, religious cult, diet, rate of metabolism, creed, and nationality or race. Even when he was crusted with the mud and blood of battle or raunchy and festered with leeches or ringworm, the women in the hamlets simply wouldn't leave him alone. When not fending off sexual attacks, E.F. manipulated with the skill of an orchestra leader the one and only M60 they had left for the remainder of this mission. They were two men short as well. Lost both in a firefight the day before at the base of Monkey Mountain. That was the first day of fighting in a search and destroy mission called OPERATION: Screaming Monkey.

The person at USARV Headquarters Operations G3 unit who came up with that mission name must have not only had an in-depth knowledge of the area where the operation was to take place but must also have had a truly distinctive and warped sense of humor. For it seemed that, at every turn, one of them touched a branch or brushed up against a tree trunk or broke a twig with one of their boots as they continued to move up the side of the mountain. Each act set off a new round of screams from the invisible monkeys hidden amongst the canopy above them. The damned noise was driving them all dinky dau. They'd been on this search and destroy shit for two days without any let up from the rain or the heat or those frigging monkeys. They were half way up Monkey Mountain and very, very, very jumpy. Promised Land made a sharp turn in the trail. His sawed-off twelve gauge single barrel shotgun exploded. A shrill chorus of monkeys surrounded them until they could hear nothing but monkeys and Promised Land's shotgun continuing to explode round after round beyond the blind curve ahead of them.

* * * * *

Al down shifted the jeep and blew his horn as he approached the blind curve just before Drake's Seat. Iree Gumbs waved at him from the pull-off overlooking Drake's Passage on the Atlantic side of St. Thomas as the jeep rounded the curve and slowed almost to a stop just off the road. Sir Frances himself had looked out from this same spot, out over this passage which he had sailed and which also bore his name.

Iree eased into the jeep's shotgun seat in the moment the jeep actually stopped before continuing back out onto the road before any other traffic could round the blind curve. He knew how Al hated to get behind other vehicles on this road. It was so hard to pass.

He was much taller and leaner than Moses, but he was his older brother's twin in looks and even in the kinds of nervousness they each seemed to exude when something was troubling them and they tried to hide it. And something was definitely bothering Iree...bad! Iree--whose given name was Henry--got his nickname because of the neatly plaited pigtails he wore his hair in most of the time. Even though they were not technically locks, like Rastafari locks which are not plaited at all but matted together (traditionally, some say, with seaweed), his friends, neighbors, acquaintances, fellow band members all began calling him Iree because that's what the Rastas say for "happy", and Henry Gumbs did always seem to be happy.

The Rastas were an international movement basically religio-political in nature, which held that Halie Selasie, the late Emperor of Ethiopia, was the holy emissary of God, come to earth to save the chosen people, the black people. Most of the followers of this faith were young and radical, but it was a growing movement full of musicians like Bob Marley and organic vegetable farmers like Ras Ujamma I, leader of the Rastafari on St. Thomas and in the Virgin Islands. He liked the connection. So Henry Gumbs let the nickname stick. He ascribed to the basic doctrines, maintained close ties with Ujamma I's community on the West End near Botany Bay, and he felt sure it would be good for the band. After all, he and his band the Gumbies were the new kids on the block, the youngest band in the Virgin Islands. They had the audacity to be different, to play mixed sets including a lot of raggae, a smattering of calypso and sooka and even some rock 'n roll and blues. For what was supposed to be an island brass band that certainly was not traditional. The Gumbies, after less than one year in existence, were booked solid for the next two years due basically to the combined efforts of Iree Henry Gumbs and Alfred Crist. They were working for good money on a regular basis and moving fast toward the big time with a recent album contract.

Most important for Iree was that, right now, the East End Bay Resort gig kept their music and playing sharp, paid the bills and provided them with a unique opportunity to play new tunes for all kinds of audiences both tourist and local, to test the songs so to speak. Iree Gumbs liked to test things out, from songs to friendships. He maintained careful records on paper or in his memory, whichever seemed appropriate to him at a given time and for a given situation. His memory was as impeccable a record of the actual as were any number of pieces of paper, for Iree was blessed, or cursed as he sometimes thought, with what might be referred to as "total recall." Recalling something was like entering an instant library. First, the title and/or author or something else to trigger the memory. Second, the page or general portion of the article or book being sought. Third, the entire section or page seemed to appear in his mind so that he could, in effect, read it as if it were in his hands.

Iree had learned very young how to put his talent to good use. He sailed through school with A's. Heaped up one scholarship on top of another award upon another honor. After all, he thought, the Virgin Islands really needed to have some heroes coming from its youth. The society cried out for leaders and righteous men from among those who would someday soon rule. He would be able to give them at least that and reap all of the benefits and rewards for himself that came with such notoriety and responsibility. Through his music he knew he could gain all of the respect and dignity denied him and his family in his youth because they were not from the old island families like the Buschultes and Baas and Paiewonskys. He could tell the story of his people during his time. He could tell the story of how much they had all suffered and how long they had waited for freedom. A line, a musical phrase or two, of the raggae-based title song of their up-coming album danced through his head as he glanced over at the co-author of that song and most of the songs to appear on the new album, his bother's best buddy in Vietnam...and now his too.

"Morning, mon."

"Morning, mon, morning." Iree smiled a toothsome smile, which covered his face as he grasped Al's hand with both of his despite the heavy weight he carried inside, the terrible concern he had to share with Al. It was the kind of natural smile Iree Gumb's was able to use to charm the audiences every evening at the East End Resort. He studied Al's face for some hint about what was happening since yesterday's craziness. Nothing. But, that wasn't unusual. Al never had been easy to read anyway. But somehow--and Iree never claimed to understand how--this Continental newsman had a deep-rooted sense of the same fears, the same frustrations, the same aspirations and dreams as he and his people had. "Me-son," he wagged his head. "My jeep, she be mashup, me-son." Iree paused. He always seemed to fall into the vernacular of his islands when in private or around friends, though his day-to-day speech patterns reflected his long tenure at Juliard and its surrounding cultural climes rather than his youthful days in St. Thomas.

"Batt'ry be dead, me-son." Iree shrugged his well-developed shoulders like a kid.

"You know there's a helluva lot more wrong with that frigging jeep of yours." Al broke off, shaking his head. They'd been through all this before many times to no avail. Iree seemed wedded to that damned jeep. "Where'd you leave it this time?"

"Okay. Ah . . . over by Mafolie."

"Oh, right. A wreck with a view of the harbor a tourist would envy?"

* * * * *

The monkeys had hardly quit screeching when the frigging mortars hit. "Incoming!" Promised Land screamed. "Incoming!" He was right on that too.

E.F., Stinky, Poet, and Al sank as deep into that forest floor as was humanly possible and snuggled up against the biggest, strongest tree trunks they could locate without taking some kind of survey. For an eternity that in real time was about four or five minutes they made like moles while the rounds hailed down on them making lumber out of the trees around them. Fires flared up at every turn. It was times like these that Al greatly envied those blind creatures that lived beneath the earth for their abilities to dig deep and dig fast.

Stinky was dead and buried under a few dozen feet of loam churned up by a couple of mortar rounds which nearly hit him in the head simultaneously. E.F.'s face was sausage but he was still alive. Hell, Al didn't know what to do for him for Christ sake. In Basic Training they hadn't told him what to do when a face was suddenly turned into sausage right in front of his eyes. So Al hit him up with a serrette of morphine until he was able to haul E.F. out of there. It stopped E.F. from hurting, if nothing else. It also knocked him out pretty good for awhile, but he bled worse. Hell, everything was a trade off. At least it shut up his frigging crying about seeing Promised Land ascending into heaven during the barrage. He kept screaming it--screeching like the goddamned monkeys-- and pointing toward the smoldering treetops surrounding them until he finally passed out from the morphine.

Poet was still holding down the flank and protecting Al's ass as usual. His BAR blazed again and again. There was a break in the fire. "Okay, Poet?"

"I'll live, Sarge. No bullet them gooks make has got my name on it, Sarge. You can take that there to the Chase Manhattan, Sarge, and get five percent on it!" He cackled.

When the cackling broke off, Al was almost certain he heard sobbing. "Promised Land?" Al could only whisper in a rasping voice. He was concerned not to speak too loudly. There might be VC mopping up after that mortar barrage. "Promised Land?" Al scoured the area in front of the squad where Promised Land had first yelled the alert and then hit the dirt. "Promised Land?"

"Hell, Sarge, he ascended into heaven. Didn't you hear what silver screen star Errol Flynn Brown was saying before you hit him up with that dope?"

"Cut the shit, Poet! Promised Land's just MIA!"

* * * * *

The battery being dead beyond the point of resurrection by jumper cables or divine intervention wasn't the only problem Iree Gumbs had with his ancient jeep. It was rusting out so badly that the place where the battery was supposed to be mounted was ready to crumble at the slightest provocation. That was the price you paid for living in such proximity to the sea. Iree knew that. Al knew that. Only the fact that Iree's jeep was known to the island folks kept it safe when he left it on the side of the road like this. Someone else's jeep or car would have ended up as just another of those gutted wrecks that littered the roadside. First, they're stripped by thieves. Then, rusted in the salt air. Soon, covered by thick growths of bush. Invaded by cacti. And finally scrap for the Bovoni landfill over by the racetrack. It just seemed such a twist for Iree's jeep, which had for years been a rolling catastrophe just waiting to take place, to collapse today of all days.

Jesus, Al thought. I have to hold it together every frigging day. Is it asking too frigging much of our jeeps abandoned on the side of the roads to do the same? But, no! "People are going to have to get used to Iree and a new jeep, me-son. You can't keep driving this death trap."

"So," Iree smirked, because he knew he was about to change the subject. He'd been island patient waiting for Al to say something . . . anything . . . about his urgent call earlier. He sensed that Al was troubled. But, he just couldn't wait any longer. In his regular English, he began. "What's all this about VILA, Al?"

"They threatened me, mon, as you know. First it was a note in my PO box. Then the attack on Remembrance. This morning an assassin attacked me at the end of my run. They're either trying to kill or kidnap me, and I don't care which at this point." Al pulled the crumpled gray scrap of paper from his shirt pocket and shoved it at Ras. "This is the note they sent me!"

Iree stared at the piece of gray paper as though it were blank at first. He knew those brothers and sisters in VILA. They were militant, yes. Damned right they were! Any people who'd been allowing themselves to be so trampled on for so long had a right--no, a responsibility--to be militant. Just read the Declaration of Independence. The song they'd written together last week seemed to flood his thoughts.

O-pres-sion. O-pres-sion.
I see it in the faces
I read it in the paintings
at our lo-cal pla-ces.
O-pression. O-pres-sion.

First, it was the traders
come to Af-ri-ca to steal us
and the tri-bal leaders who,
with-out guilt, sell us.
Chains be chains, me brothers.
Chains be chains, me sisters.

64

Whether forged by oth-ers
or by our own leaders.

O-pres-sion. O-pres-sion.
I see it in our faces
I read it in the paintings
at our lo-cal pla-ces.
O-pres-sion. O-pres-sion.

"This is the same color paper, the same style of lettering, everything is the same, Al."

"The same as what, Iree?"

"The same as the notes the Governor received yesterday and the Senate President received late last night when he called you at the club . . . both by special courier."

"How do you know that?"

"Well, Teddy told you about his last night, and Wadabli told me about the Governor's note. Now, I've seen yours, too. All the same, me-son. All the same."

"Except the message."

"Yes, mon. They threatened to assassinate the Governor and the Senate President during Carnival."

"That's right. Now that sounds pretty serious to me, doesn't it to you?"

"It must be some kind of trick." His brothers and sisters could not be involved in such a bloodthirsty plot. Change through education and election. That had always been the goal of VILA, ever since he had helped draft the "Haul-over Resolution". Not change through violence, and especially not violence against one of the powerful members of the system who had helped them so much over the years to be heard as a group for forceful and valid change--through the system not through violence. They had gained a lot of the political power they now had primarily because Al, as a dedicated journalist and idealist, believed they had the right of any other group, to be heard without prejudice, and what they had to say was worth saying. He had felt VILA's message of hope, of change for the young and change for the better, was a good one, one which challenged the principle of democracy he believed in and was willing to take a career and political risk for because of his beliefs. He had taken VILA on as a legitimate news story to follow as part of his on-going series of dispatches concerning the Virgin Islands and the Caribbean. But this note Iree was staring at in his own hands pretty well indicated that those same people, VILA, were going to murder this man if he interfered with their frigging revolution. And the signature. Ras Ujamma I. It sure looked like their leader's handwriting all right. Still he had not been in on any discussion of such things as this and he just couldn't believe that any of his brothers and sisters would do any such thing without talking to him first.

"I don't want to believe any of this shit, you know!" Al shoved his fists into his pockets for a few seconds as he fought back hard bitter tears. Then he was cracking his knuckles trying to control the growing anger, the sense of betrayal he felt choking him. "I really don't."

"I simply can't believe it, Al." Iree wagged his head. "I must find out what the hell's going on here."

"Jesus, you know, maybe they're somehow being manipulated . . . you know, set up by the U.S. to stage this whole thing? Without even being aware that they're being manipulated."

"I'm going to prove to you that VILA's not responsible for all this. This whole thing just stinks."

"I know, me-son. It stinks of company perfume."

Iree shrugged somewhat uneasily, glancing at the crumpled piece of gray paper in his hand. "I know the facts look pretty bleak, Al."

"Damn, me-son. You know I hope we can prove that, or maybe it was just a conspiracy to force Ras Ujamma I and his family into joining forces with the revolutionaries simply because he was already being identified with them." Al too glanced at the paper Iree still gripped between his fingers like a salamander that was trying to wriggle away. "But."

"You know I'm going to do my best, mon."

Al took one more look under the hood of Ras' jeep, more as some kind of formality than anything else. The jeep was trashed and they both knew it. He shook his head and dropped the hood down gingerly. "I really think we're going to have to write an obituary for this old baby. Guess you'll have to ride with me until we get a chance to meet up with Lois. She took off on an assignment already this morning."

"If you say so, but I think Lois and me should do most of the investigating on this mess anyway. You need to be figuring out this damned scenario and writing it all down."

"What the hell do you mean . . . you do all the investigating?"

"Don't argue, mon. I mean, Lois and me haven't received threatening notes or been attacked by an armada or been assaulted by an assassin. Have we?"

"Well."

BEEP. BEEP. BEEP. "Hey guys! What's happening here? Your jeep finally die on you, Mr. Gumbs?"

"Lois?" Al--and most people who lived on the islands--never ceased to be amazed at this particular phenomenon. Whenever you would think of someone hard enough or just really needed to see them, they somehow showed up. You would run across them at a bar or a restaurant or on Main Street or, like now, they just come driving by when they're needed and either they spot you or you spot them. It sure made things easier all the way around even if you couldn't explain it.

"What'cha doing here, Daughter?" Iree chuckled. "Thought you were on an important information-gathering mission?"

"Mission accomplished!" Lois shoved her gear lever into Park, reached between her legs and produced several sheets of paper, waving them at the boys. "Well, it's all top secret stuff . . . the Carnival list!" she giggled. "So it turns out, an old publishing buddy of mine, Les Trane, is the Chairman of Carnival." She grinned. "Small world, huh?"

They both nodded.

"Anyway, he was able to get a copy of the list for me, but he recommends discretion. Word travels fast in the troupe sub-culture, according to Les."

"Great!" Al leaped to the car and planted a quick kiss on her flushed cheek. "That's just great, Lois!"

"Okay, Al. I take your jeep, check out the musicians and bands."

67

"And VILA and the West End Commune?"

"Yes. Definitely."

"Okay. Maybe they'll meet with Teddy and Esteban . . . maybe myself or you if needed. The politicians'll probably balk at that. At you for sure. At me, maybe or maybe not."

"I'll check it all out, me-son. You go with Lois. She can take you out to the East End to the yacht. You can lay sort of low for awhile and work on the story and communicating with everybody involved. You know, D.C., local pols, me, Lois. Right Lois?"

"Absolutely, Iree. Absolutely!" Lois nodded vigorously. "You haven't heard from Santurce yet. That's important for you to follow up on, Al. Most important."

"And you're the only one of us who can put this thing together. What happens if they do kidnap or kill you? What then? What then?"

"Maybe. Maybe you're right. I just don't like it." But first we'll go talk this list over with Georges. He organized those parades for years, before Les Trane. Probably knows just about every troupe by heart. He'll sure know how to eliminate names from this list."

"And we'll sure as hell need that kind of help," Lois giggled, pointing at the list she held in her left hand. "There must be more than a hundred entries on this damned list."

"Cheese'n'bread, me-son, and only two days to find the right one."

"Only one copy, Lois?"

"Yeah."

"No problem, mon. Iree has a copy in his head already." Iree laughed as he gave his old jeep a final pat on the front fender.

"So do I," Lois grinned and tapped her forehead. "So do I."

CHAPTER 6
PETER ISLAND

10:37 a.m.

"Cast off the bow line, Frenchie!" Al stood with his legs spread apart slightly behind the boat's wheel--teak with brass trim that was kept gleaming by Mister Tommy Bryan better known as Frenchie.

Schooners, ketches, catamarans, and trimarans crammed the small boat basin carved out of the coral and volcanic rock by the sea over centuries. Their halyards rang in the stiff breeze. The basin water appeared dark and somewhat opaque in contrast to the quartz-like clarity of the sea beyond the channel that connected the basin to the Atlantic Ocean. Across the white and azure water lay the islands of Yost Van Dyke, Tortola, and St. John-- shaggy green lumps floating on the sea. Far down the archipelago lay the shaggy green lump that was the original home of Frenchie's branch of the Bryans.

His Bryans lived in an area just off of Charlotte Amalie harbor called Estate Honduras or French Town. It had originally been populated by French islanders from St. Barths who were primarily fishermen by trade. Most of them had relatives over on the North Side where the French people who settled there, also from St. Barths, were farmers. Frenchie Bryan's family was from a long line of fishermen. His grandfather and grandmother had come to St. Thomas looking for more opportunity and for a chance to get under the American flag. They constructed a little shanty in Estate Honduras right by the water where their small, oar-and-sail-driven fishing skiff was beached.

"Aye, Cap'n!" Frenchie replied smartly as he finished neatly coiling the aft line before going forward to cast that line off. Properly coiled lines were the sign of a good ship, and nobody got hurt that way, Frenchie always said. He prided himself in the fact that Remembrance was the pride of St. Thomas and probably of all the Virgin Islands. The brass was always spit polished. The teak decking always gleamed. Everything was "spic'n span." And them engines ran like twin charms.

The twin Perkins diesels purred under the throttle, clear aqua water gurgling up from beneath the hull from the underwater exhausts as Al made ready to take Remembrance into the Atlantic. He didn't like this shit at all. He had a lot of trouble fighting the growing feeling that he was somehow running out on this investigation and this story, leaving his friends to take the chances. First, it was Iree and Lois. And when he showed up at Water Sports Center even Frenchie got into his shit. They all told him the same thing. It's ridiculous to risk being out front on this one. "You'll be too exposed!" Lois had pressed. Georges nodded as he served the espresso earlier. "You're the only one who can write this story."

"Okay, Cap'n. Take her out, me-boy! Slow and easy." Frenchie howled as he coiled the bowline carefully onto the teak deck.

Al eased down on the throttle and steered the motor yacht clear of the dockage out into the short channel which had been cut by the resort management to connect the small bay area where they built the Water Sports Center and Marina to the Atlantic Ocean. The bay had been separated from the ocean by a haul over--a sand shoal one literally had to haul a boat over in order to be able to continue by sea. But that had to be dealt with when management decided to build the marina to service the resort and add to its attractiveness to both tourists and local residents looking for a lovely place to live. No one, especially tourists coming to St. Thomas, would be very excited about having to take hold of 15-20 thousand pounds of sailboat and drag it across twenty-five feet of coral sand called a haul over.

Al obeyed the "no wake" rule which had been put in place by the management since the haul over had been adequately dealt with so that even power yachts as large as Remembrance could come and go easily. Frenchie obeyed the rule carefully as well. So did the other boat people who understood the importance of not knocking others' boats around just because they wanted to go fast. Certainly there were those few "hot shots" who would come down from the States to work at the Water Sports Center and Marina or to charter their own boats out of the marina that pushed the rule just to the limits. Sometimes they'd misjudge and throw a huge wake over the entire basin. Occasionally sailboats and motor yachts were damaged, usually minor damage from one boat glancing against another or a boat banging up against the dock harder than it should. When this happened, if the culprits worked for the marina or for the East End Bay

Resorts management, they were fired on the spot. If not, they would be banned from the marina permanently.

Frenchie beamed as he entered the Pilot House easing himself into the Captain's Chair behind the wheel and nudging Al out of the way. "I'll take 'er now, Cap'n. You need to get below decks and do your writin', now don't ya?"

"Yeah, Frenchie. You're right. Take her out of the channel and hold a course for Peter Island. We'll have a snack at the club after I've finished."

"Right ya are, Cap'n." His bulbous nose glowed red as did his aging leather-like cheeks.

Frenchie really loves these little excursions, Al chuckled as he made his way down the ladder that led from the Pilot House to his command and work center below decks. Al did most of his writing on Remembrance, usually anchored in some quiet, deserted island cove or with Frenchie at the helm like now. Only occasionally did he try to control the boat from his duplicate control panel below. It was too dangerous because he would lose concentration on the course of the boat when he got into his writing. It was sort of like the rumor he had once heard about Gary Trudeaux creating Doonesberry strips in airplanes. He had never been able to confirm that rumor, but he knew for sure that he did his work on the yacht.

He pulled the hatch shut and eased himself into the Captain's chair covered in royal blue leatherette, which was permanently installed on a stainless pedestal in front of his computer/word processor station. He sucked in a deep breath as Remembrance cleared the channel. He could tell because as Frenchie steered the yacht into the open sea, he hit the throttle a little harder. Al checked his receiver to make sure it was making proper contact with home base. Santurce's call would have to be patched to the boat from the villa. Two-way patches were a little shaky. He switched on his computer and dialed up the villa computer via modem. He logged in. Linked the modem and the computer. That way, when Santurce called, he'd be immediately alerted and could patch in and receive the call or message.

This story was still in the making. But all that three years of experience he had in his head could provide some super background. That should not only make it more interesting but also make solving the problem for "Who done it?" a little easier. He began typing background. He moved across the keyboard as if he were doing with it the same kind of automatic writing his favorite poet and political hero William Butler Yeats had done more than half a century before with his pen and paper. Yeats would take pen in hand and, as the spirits moved his hand, that pen would write the words on the paper in front of him without him even realizing what he was writing. Al, instead, clicked away at a computer terminal on-board his yacht Remembrance of Things Past sending electronic signals across the Caribbean Sea and the Atlantic Ocean, over the east coast to Doc Streeter's New York City computers.

<<<BACKGROUND ON "CARNIVAL COUP D'ETAT>>>

Most Americans know that once a year at the start of the Lenten Season, New Orleans goes a little berserk. The streets become one big series of parties and parades culminating in the biggest bash and parade this side of Rio. In fact, the Mardi Gras which started out as strictly a "blow-it-out-before-lent festival", has become so popular and so economically profitable for New Orleans that many other cities in the States are emulating their success. A good example is the Winter Fest in Fort Lauderdale, which started out simply as a Christmas Parade of Boats. Over several years, it has evolved into a complete festival celebrating Christmas and the coming of the Winter Season, an economic factor to Fort Lauderdale and to all of the Florida Gold Coast.

The New Orleans or Rio of the Caribbean Islands has to be Trinidad/Tobago. It is certainly the kind of carnivals in the islands, and just about every island of any size has some kind of carnival.

The United States Virgin Islands is no exception. In fact, as a territory, it is more fortunate than most Caribbean countries. It has three carnivals-- one for each of its three main islands: St. Croix, St. John, and St. Thomas. Christmas season on St. Croix, Emancipation Day on St. John, and "Rosatime!" and "Jump up!" in St. Thomas in the late spring after tourist season is over. As one well-known politician and media personality put it, "It allows us to let off steam. In a small, insular island society like ours, if we don't let it out, there's no telling what might happen." So once a year, shortly after the Easter Season, Thomians blow it out with their carnival where they also crown the only "Calypso King of the World."

Everyone's guard is down. It's a time when we are all brothers and sisters.

<<<BACKGROUND ON "CARNIVAL COUP D'ETAT">>>

72

The VP knows this well enough and seems to be ready to capitalize on the carnival atmosphere to cover the coup until after it hits with the force of a surprise hurricane.

"Cap'n? Cap'n? Yo! Cap'n?"

"Aye, Frenchie?" Al's fingers stopped in mid-motion...the caesura between the ending of one thought and the beginning of another.

"Ain't your horn working down dere?"

"No! Monitoring the villa's computer."

"Call for you from Mr. Teddy."

Al picked up his auxiliary telephone receiver. "Al Crist. Over."

"How are you guys holding up, mon? Over."

"Okay, I guess. I feel sort of out of it. Ah . . . over."

"I copy. Have a meet set with Attorney Black. You remember Edna, don't you? Over."

"Certainly. Over."

"Well, she's still VILA's attorney and still as foxy as ever. The meet is her, Ras Ujamma I, Esteban, me and you. You *have* to be there! Do you copy? Over."

"I copy. What time? Where? Over."

"5:30 p.m. sharp. Not Virgin Islands time, me-son. 5:30 on the nose or no meeting!"

Static hovered in the receiver.

"Remember! You are a requirement!"

Static grew more insistent.

"Losing patch, Al. Over."

"I'll be there, me-son. Over and out. Al clicked off the receiver set. "Frenchie!"

"Yo, Cap'n!"

"We gotta be back at Charlotte Amalie Harbor before dark . . . by no later than 5:00 or quarter after five."

"Right ya are, Cap'n. Right ya are."

"Can you drop me at the Senate dock?"

"Negative, Cap'n. Dock not big enough or sturdy enough for Remembrance. You could dingy into it though."

"We'll see how the time goes. Gotta be at the Senate before 5:30."

Al returned to the keyboard.

<<<BACKGROUND ON "CARNIVAL COUP D'ETAT>>>

Calypso. A very special music that plays a very special part in carnivals throughout the Caribbean. In fact, every carnival from Trinidad to St. Kitts, from Antigua to St. Thomas has as a major part of its carnival a calypso competition. The competition during the tents is furious. Everyone has their favorite. Calypso tents are the battleground for calypsonians on their way to the crown. And, calypso as a musical genre is very politically oriented. Very much into social commentary type lyrics. In fact, that's a major portion of the judging in calypso competitions--the import of the lyrics. So it makes some kind of sense that one of the very greatest ever calypsonians in the Caribbean was the Mighty Chalkdust--a school teacher from Trinidad--and one of the best ever in St. Thomas, Calypso King of the World Lord Blakie, who was in real life a policeman, Kenneth Blake, Jr., past Director of the Police Athletic League (PAL). These two always clashed at the St. Thomas Calypso King of the World competition during Carnival International Tent. And each of these great performers always had scathing political commentary to make in his presentation.

<<<BACKGROUND AND LEAD ON "CARNIVAL COUP D'ETAT>>>

"Land ho, Cap'n!" Land ho! Peter Island Yacht Basin to starboard. Prepare to dock for nourishment."

"Yo, Frenchie. Let me save this shit." Peter Island. Home of Old Ben Gunn's treasure. Every time he dropped anchor here he remembered the first time he ever read *Treasure Island*. At nine years old, sitting in the corner of the public library, he had absolutely no idea where Treasure Island was, but he just knew that someday he'd go there.

Al turned his attention back to the terminal screen. "Oh, well," he shrugged. "Pick it up after lunch." He saved and exited. The machine whirred, storing everything he'd typed into the new file. The whirring stopped. Storage complete.

* * * * *

11:25 a.m.

The waveless waves lapped against barnacled pilings that held the deck above the clear sea. Banana palms bunched around the edges of the deck furthest from the pale green water. Coconut palms in huge stone and mortar planters shaded the deck.

Al almost dozed over his white wine and raw conch in lime juice and peppers appetizer as the flopping sounds of the waves against the pilings and palm fronds rattling overhead in harmony with the halyards from the docked boats seemed to hypnotize him.

"Nobody else seen dem, dat I can find," the red-skinned waiter whispered near his ear, "but some o' we did go der. Me-boy, look like bunch o' people, mon, campin' and t'ing."

The waiter had introduced himself as Gotlieb earlier when he recommended the conch, fresh from the sea that morning. He knew because he caught them. Yes, he waited tables at the yacht club, but he also fished for a living as he used to in his home island Grenada. Looking for new fishing spots carried him to the unvisited parts of Peter Island. It was on one such visit about a week ago that he and some mates saw campfires and shadowy movements on the beach on the opposite end of the island, hidden from easy view because it was in a cove that had its back to the sea so to speak thus keeping from view whatever was in the cove or on shore by its waters. The next day Gotlieb and his mates took a dinghy to the same spot and went ashore.

"We found all kind o' dis real stretchy, color papers and t'ing."

"Crepe paper," Al interjected.

"Crepe paper," Gotlieb repeated. "T'ought a journalist, like ya'self, jus' might wan' know dis. Dey was campfires . . . lots o' dem . . . crushed out." Gotlieb glanced around him. "Me take you der . . . show you. Okay?"

12:30 p.m.

Thick growths of knurled sea grape trees and palms seemed to gradually push the deserted beach into the Caribbean Sea. Its bleached white sand held fragments of a thousand footprints. Piles of charred coconut shells, pieces of dead palms, and sea grape branches were scattered along the half-mile of beach mostly under the shade of the coconut palms and sea grapes. People.

"A lot of people were here," Al whispered in Frenchie's craggy ear.

"And recently, me-son. Dey mus' be at dis site for t'ree, four days at least, Cap'n."

"You see, mon?" Gotlieb was saying. "Me boys, dey find dis kinda t'ing." He pointed at some scraps of black and gold and red crepe paper stuck on a sea grape branch. "Dey say, carnival! Dat's wha' dey say. Carnival." He smiled--two silver teeth gleamed out from the upper center of his mouth. Maybe he was old Ben Gunn with the secret of Treasure Island still stowed behind those gray eyes and silver teeth. After all, this was the island, wasn't it, that Robert Louis Stevenson called Treasure Island. Was old Ben Gunn's cave really near here? He'd never admit it, but he'd gone looking for it several times when he'd sailed to the island on his own. After all, he'd promised himself as a kid that someday he'd get to Treasure Island.

"St. Thomas be de only carnival now, mon. So." Ben Gunn Gotlieb shrugged his shoulders. "Too far, mon. St. Thomas be too far, mon, but St. Thomas be de only one, mon."

"Okay, me-son. Okay." Frenchie nodded.

Al turned away. He had to smile and didn't want to seem offensive to Gotlieb. His reasoning is crazy but probably correct. Yet why would anyone go to the trouble and expense of preparing a float for the St. Thomas carnival parades here, all the way over on Peter Island? It just doesn't make sense. Unless this group was preparing something super-secret. Like a coup d'etat perhaps? "Frenchie?"

"Yo, Cap'n."

"Got something to stash that crepe paper in?"

Frenchie's face contorted. "Wha'?"

"So we can keep it for evidence or decorating Remembrance," Al quipped. "We've gotta get going. Now!"

"Right, Cap'n. Right ya are, Cap'n." Frenchie bent over to grab samples. He'd put them in his pockets for now and stuff them into plastic bags once they were back onboard Remembrance. Back safe and sound on the sea again. Being on solid land too long gave Frenchie Bryan the creeps.

"Some say it be VILA, mon. You know VILA, mon. You write about dem before, yeah?" Gotlieb leered at them from the shadow of a cluster of sea grape trees.

"Yeah." Al watched as Frenchie fetched the crepe paper and stuffed it into his pockets.

"VILA know you, too, mon!" Gotlieb cackled. "VILA say you not make no five-t'irty meetin'. VILA say you write for dem . . . and de revolution."

"Like shit, I will."

"Oh, yes, mon. You will, Mr. Alfred Crist," Gotlieb smirked. "You will!" He signaled his men to move in from the shadows. They were led by a slightly taller and thinner dark skinned Grenadian, Fist.

"Well, Old Ben Gunn you sure as hell ain't!"

* * * * *

2:00 p.m.

"I just talked to Teddy. Iree spoke into the receiver of the only working pay phone within miles. He enunciated one word at a time, because he knew that she would never understand him if he rattled off calypso. He could hear Lois's breath catch in her throat. "He's tried to hail Al and Frenchie on every channel imaginable to delay the time of that frigging meeting between them and VILA from 5:30 to 6:00 but he hasn't been able to raise them at'all."

"Well, damnit! Let's go find them, Iree!"

"Teddy said we could use one of the government power boats. There's a 35-footer docked at Johnny Harms Marina. The Brown Pelican II. Slip number 37."

"I'll meet you there in twenty minutes."

"Okay. By the way, that troupe practicing out here and building their float in secret at Pineapple Beach is certainly legitimate enough or should I say harmless enough. Just a bunch of boat people from Red Hook area that make up one of the few troupes that are basically 'continental'."

"Okay . . . okay. Twenty minutes."

"Okay." Iree heard the click of Lois' receiver. He knew where he could get at least one rifle . . . the Chicom AK Moses had shipped home to him through the mails, piece by piece, from Vietnam. Iree remembered the letter his brother had written detailing the engagement when he and his good buddy Al Crist had captured two Chicom AK's. Al Crist sent one home a piece at a time just as Promised Land did. Al kept his in the arms compartment on Remembrance. Iree Gumbs kept his brother's cleaned and oiled at all times and wrapped in clothes soaked in linseed oil. The rifle was hidden in a box in his closet. His mother would've had a fit if she'd ever found out about the gun. She hadn't. Home was only a couple of minutes from the telephone at the French Grocery on the upper North Side. It was on the way to the East End too, where the Brown Pelican II awaited their arrival. He just felt sure that he should take the rifle with him. He had a sinking feeling that they were all going to need whatever firearms they could lay their hands on and wrap their fingers around before this mess was over.

* * * * *

2:12 p.m.

Al couldn't be sure where he was being taken. All he knew with any certainty was that he and Frenchie had been overwhelmed by twenty or more assailants, their faces and heads covered by dark hoods. They had been blindfolded and gagged. Then they were separated. He didn't know what happened to Frenchie. All he knew for sure was that he, himself, had been transported by dinghy to some other place. He wasn't even sure, however, where that was or how far he'd traveled. He did remember a long dingy ride over some pretty choppy water. But, somewhere along the way, someone had popped him with a knock-out shot. It had put him out like a snuffed hurricane lamp. His last thought had been of how he was going to miss Santurce's call . . . and the meeting at 5:30.

* * * * *

3:00 p.m.

Juan Santurce did not call. He sent an electronic mail message instead.

<<<ELECTRONIC MAIL MESSAGE: TOP SECRET LINE: SEND>>>

THE HAMLET'S HOT, SHAKESPEARE. MUST

MACBETH THIS ONE. SORRY!

SANTURCE

<<<ELECTRONIC MAIL MESSAGE: TOP SECRET LINE:
END>>>

* * * * *

3:22 p.m.

The Brown Pelican II idled alongside Remembrance as Iree Gumbs looped two holding lines over her--one at the bow, the other astern. In the flat water just off Drake's Channel, the she seemed lifeless, deserted.

"Okay, Lois. Shut she down!" Iree straddled the stern of the Chris Craft 35-foot cabin cruiser owned by the Virgin Islands government.

"Aye, Captain." Lois closed the throttle down. The diesel inboards went quiet. The sea around them was also quiet. So quiet in fact that Lois felt suddenly very uneasy. It wasn't like Al or Frenchie to leave the yacht completely unattended or unprotected like this.

"Hold tight, daughter. I boarding she . . . see wha' I cyan see."

Lois didn't answer. Iree, for some reason, had lapsed totally into dialect with her. She figured it was an indication that he felt comfortable with her. She only hoped she could understand him okay. She fingered the rifle Iree had given her. She'd never really held a rifle before. He'd called it an AK-47 assault rifle. "Used in Vietnam." The gun was like new--clean and smelling strongly of linseed oil. She'd found nothing at the villa that they could use.

"Lois! Come, mon. Quick!" Iree's voice ripped through the stillness of the flat and breezeless sea.

She nearly jumped out of her skin--like a jumbie crossed her shadow. Not so much the sound of his voice breaking the silence but more the urgency of his tone. She hesitated just for a moment. What was the situation on Remembrance? Did Iree need help? She turned slightly to her right almost as if pulled by some magnet. She was looking directly down the barrel of Iree's AK-47. She faltered, then scooped it up on her way out the door.

* * * * *

3:27 p.m.

80

Lois slipped down the ladder from the Pilot's Cabin above Iree. She carried his AK locked and loaded ready to fire like soldiers she had seen in TV war footage. In her camouflage fatigues, she looked like G.I. Josephine. The boat seemed deserted, but she knew Iree was on board . . . at least. About half way down the ladder, she sensed something, someone. "Okay, here goes nothing," she muttered. "And . . . everything." She leaped down the ladder brandishing her weapon. "EEEAAAHHH . . . EEEAAAHHH!"

The lump of a person who was trying to tie Iree up with some fishing line whirled as he heard her screams. Lois instinctively lashed across his jaw with the butt of the rifle she squeezed in her hand. Blood shot out from between his lips. Teeth flew across the cabin, tic-tacing against the bulkhead like stray bullets. As the man careened to the floor, collapsing in a jumble of limbs and fish line, Lois circled the cabin searching for any others. Her pulsed raced. Her heart banged right through her skin out into the air of the cabin. She was sure that Iree could hear it, even *see* it, as she finally bent over him and pulled a wad of paper towels out of his mouth.

He spit fragments of paper, coughed. "Dere be nobody else on below, daughter. No one."

"Nothing fore or aft, either Iree." She grinned. "I checked before coming down to rescue you." Her grin exploded. "Me-son."

"Check de mon, Lois." Iree struggled with the fiber line that the man on the floor had successfully wrapped around his wrists but not had time to tighten. "See if he be holdin' somet'ing . . . some clue."

Lois rolled the man over with her foot and bent over him rifling his pockets. "Nothing." She felt a scrap of paper in his left front trouser pocket. "Except this scrap of paper." Lois handed him the piece of crumpled gray paper. "It's the same."

Without looking directly at her, Iree glanced at the paper in her hand. Yes. The same color. He nodded. Yes. The same damned gray. Scribbled on the piece of paper were three words, which he read as he slipped the paper from between Lois' trembling fingers. "The Old Danish Warehouse."

"You think . . . ?"

"I t'ink dere's a good chance."

81

"That they're there?"

"Could be." Iree looked around. Lois was crying. He reached out to her. "Yes, daughter. It could be and we gonna find out for sure." She crumpled into his arms, the AK sling sliding down her arm and the weapon clattering to the floor as she moved. "It's okay, Lois. Okay."

After a few moments, Iree began to pull away, forcing Lois to stand-alone again. She stooped to pick up the fallen weapon.

"In de Army dat would've cost you fifty push ups at least, daughter," he tried to joke.

"How would you know?" she sniffled. "YOU weren't ever in."

"Al told me . . . and my brother."

Lois nodded. A pinched smile wrinkled the corners of her lips.

"Lois, you be great earlier. De way you come down dat ladder screaming bloody murder and waving dat rifle. If I hadn't known better, I'd've t'ought you were leadin' a full-fledged boardin' party!"

"Shit. I didn't know what else to do. When I heard you calling me, I just got scared as all hell. So I said to myself, if Iree is in trouble, then my coming in strongly would be helpful. If you weren't in any trouble, then what would it hurt? I'd just look like a complete fool. You know what I mean?"

"Yes, daughter. I do." Iree patted her on the rump. "You sure saved my ass, I know dat. De creep come in on me not two seconds after I be callin' for you to come aboard."

"I'm just glad I was in time."

"Hey, you and me bot'. So, what we be waitin' for?"

"Yeah, let's get going and find Al and Frenchie!"

"Better leave Remembrance here for now. Let's secure her . . . and get de prisoner. Maybe, somehow, dey might still get back here and need her. You and me'll take Brown Pelican II and the prisoner." Iree was climbing the ladder behind Lois to the Pilot's Cabin as he rambled on, issuing orders. "We'll give de mon to de police in Charlotte Amalie." There was no time to lose.

CHAPTER 7

THE OLD DANISH WAREHOUSE

5:45 p.m.

Lois couldn't get that scene at the East End Bay Resort Restaurant out of her mind, especially now, after what they'd found near Peter Island and on Remembrance. She could still see poor old Georges slouching toward their table when they arrived shortly after Iree dropped them off. Georges carried a single rose in a cut glass vase just as he had last night when she and Al had finally met in person. He presented it to them with tears welled up in his hazel eyes. The rose was crushed to a shapeless pulp. Hanging from the neck of the vase on a red ribbon was a gray card bearing the letters VILA scribbled in blood. Al had been shaken to his chi. She could tell that it had been deeply disturbing, leaving him what he called "double balanced" or vulnerable.

"I'm so very sorry for zhis, Monsieur Alfred," Georges wept. He had bitten his lower lip so hard Lois thought he would bite right through it. "But zhese scoundrels with zheir dreaded locks." He shrugged with impotence. "What else could I do? Zhey said zhey would kill me on zhe spot if I did not deliver zhis message to you when you showed up today. How did zhose people know you would be here? Those rascal rastas. Zhey *would* kill me, Monsieur Alfred. You know zhey would!"

She feared for Al's life now more than ever. Jumbies still ran up and down her spine thinking about it, even as she and Iree approached the Old Danish Warehouse near the market. The Oriental Troupe, which was listed as using the warehouse, was a brand new troupe. Nobody seemed to know anything about it. A logical suspect, then, in a situation where most troupes exist from year to year and act almost like social clubs during the non-carnival times of year for the locals. The building in front of them now was one of those few old Danish warehouses which survived the two major fires in St. Thomas in the 1800's and had eluded the renovation efforts of Jews from New York, Indians from India, South Americans from Colombia or Arabs from Pakistan. It still remained as it had originally been structured.

83

The workmanship was meticulous in the way the red, brown, and yellow stones were pieced together with a sprinkling of brain coral here and or fan coral there as well as old bricks and anything else the Danes could scrounge to create the massive thick walls. Sometimes you might even find pieces of elk horn in the walls looking like fossils trapped by the masons as they worked. The "whatever you can scrounge" syndrome was certainly typical of this insular society where everything had to be imported, often even the sand that was used to make the mortar and cement.

The masonry of carefully laid stones didn't seem to be particularly typical of the West Indian culture of today in the Virgin Islands, Lois mused. They seemed to be careful about very little. Yet, the workmen who masoned this building so many years before had been damned careful about how they built their walls . . . even to the way they made their mortar. Those old West Indian masons mixed a mortar out of crushed coral, sand, and molasses. This seemingly bizarre mixture had held those walls in place against the onslaught of some of the worst storms in the history of the islands including the cataclysmic combination of earthquake, tidal wave, hurricane, and fires which devastated St. Thomas and sank the British Royal Mail Carrier, the HMS Rhone. That ship now serves as one of the most favored and visited dive spots in the islands . . . just off of Salt Island along Drake's Channel. That wasn't far from Peter Island which some say was Robert Louis Stevenson's Treasure Island. What kind of treasure had Al and Frenchie stumbled upon there that would cause them to be abducted . . . and maybe worse . . . she hated the thought . . . killed? Lois shuddered.

Pieces of mortar crumbled under Iree's touch as he tried to pull himself up on the ledge of the window just beside the alley entrance that they'd found padlocked from the outside. A two-inch thick hurricane shutter made of wood was partially closed over the window opening. It was attached to the stone wall by wrought iron hinges. Once they had been painted black. After a good deal of effort, Iree was able to use sheer upper body strength to pull himself up enough so that he could rest his elbows on the window ledge. Holding on with his right arm, he gradually worked the shutter open enough to allow him to crawl through the opening. "Jesus!" he muttered down at Lois as the inner darkness began to gradually give up its secrets as the sunlight streamed in through the window. "What a friggin' mess, mon."

"What? What did you say, Iree?"

He reached down for her hand. "Careful, daughter. Dis wall's sorta crumblin'."

84

* * * * *

Al struggled from a drugged sleep only to find himself bound and gagged with adhesive tape and staring straight up at a shard of light on the ceiling of a building. The light splinter looked just like the shard of a rubber tree that impaled Promised Land's bandana halfway up another rubber tree. He concentrated on that light, summoning focus. Gradually, he reached deep inside his chi for patience, control, and energy. He knew that he must escape his bonds . . . somehow. He had no knife or other cutting edge. He was still too stupored to see much in the darkness. Anyway, he had no idea what might await him within the confines of these stone walls. Staying put was definitely in order.

So, he was left with his principles and their applications. His third eye seemed to suddenly seize control. His brain rushed with electric like energy. He began to chant and slowly twist his wrists back and forth and sideways, always twisting one wrist away from the other, never attempting to tear the tape, only stretching the adhesive little by little.

* * * * *

At first he wasn't sure from so far away, but he thought that twenty feet above his head, pinned to the trunk of a wild rubber tree by a shard of lumber that had just moments ago been a tree itself was Promised Land's beaded headband made out of a bandana. Or at least it sure as hell looked like it from where Al was standing, half-way up Monkey Mountain below the second canopy of a rain forest area that had just felt the firey fist of war in its fecund gut. The monkeys were finally quieting down. No VC had showed yet to mop up. No more mortar rounds incoming. As he stared at the blue-and-yellow-and-red object dangling from the slab of wood that struck the rubber tree like a spike, he was trying to hail HQ on the radio. He held the receiver in his hand. The radio pack was welded to Stinky's back, but somehow it still worked. It sounded like it worked anyway . . . plenty of static. Al couldn't raise his company commander, Captain Charger. He also couldn't find hide nor hair of Promised Land. He seemed to actually have ascended into heaven just like E.F. had announced.

Captain Charger was a self-made bootstrap Captain, possessing not even a high school diploma until he managed to eke out his GED. He was a Korean vet. Airborne. Ranger. Kit Carson and LRRP during his first tour in Nam. Only with that degree could he become an officer and a gentleman. He'd been a grunt. He couldn't just leave them up here like this unreinforced and down to two men left fighting, one wounded ground sausage, one KIA, and one ascending out of action . . .

"Hurdy Gurdy, this is Screaming Monkey one. Do you read me? Over!" Through the static and the incessant waves of monkey chatter, the voice was clearly that of Captain Charger himself.

Al tore his eyes from the object dangling from the tree and stared at the radio receiver in his hand. It works! "Screaming Monkey one. This is Hurdy Gurdy A-1-A. We have an emergency situation here, sir. Over."

"HOLD! I REPEAT!" the Captain screamed into Al's ear. "HOLD your position at all costs, Sergeant Crist!" Captain Charger's voice stopped for a moment. Static filled the void. Monkeys screamed sporadically around him. Stinky was starting to smell already. This fucking jungle. That was what did it. If you sit too long in one place you start rotting, even though you're still more or less alive . . . "And I mean at *all* costs!" Each word was a bullet into his and Poet's bodies. Al winced.

"But, Captain Charger, sir. Begging the Captain's pardon, sir. But I don't think the Captain fully realizes my situation here, sir. We lost two KIA yesterday, sir."

"Sergeant!"

"Sir?"

"Hold your position. That's an order!"

"And just now we've got one MIA that ascended up a rubber tree into heaven, we think, and one KIA whose got the radio pack welded to his back. I wonder if they'll be able to get his body into a body bag and still allow me to be in communication with Company HQ, sir?"

"HOLD, SERGEANT! HOLD!"

"And one badly wounded. His face is like sausage, sir, you know? But he *is* alive, sir. You can bet your ass on that, sir! We can save him, sir. If you'll just get us the fuck out of here, sir. We're all that's left of a whole fucking platoon, sir, and we're facing a goddamned company of NVA regulars it looks like, sir."

As Al breathed, there was only static on the radio. Maybe the captain was being swayed? "At least get my wounded man out of here, sir. There's only *two* of us left to fight off fucking Company A of the First NVA Regiment!"

"The order stands," filtered through the static. "Hold your position, Sergeant--*at all costs*!"

"But, sir, my wounded?"

"If anybody in this fucking Battalion can do it, Crist, you and, I'll bet Whitman, can. God be with you both! Good luck! Over and out!"

The static that time was final. Al's vision crawled back up that rubber tree to where Promised Land's headband was still impaled on its trunk by a single spike of wood. How the fuck did Charger know that the other man left was Poet?

* * * * *

5:50 p.m.

The shard of light on the ceiling of the Old Danish Warehouse danced and finally exploded into a huge rectangle of sunshine, illuminating a small portion of the inside wall. Al could hear crumbling stones and mortar falling from around the opening window shutter. On the wall hung a poster from the very first carnival in 1912.

What a time that carnival must have been . . . a time without political upheavals when Carmen Nicholson and Leo Sibilly were elected as Carnival Queen and King respectively and, after nearly two days of horse racing, water pageants, historical dramas about the island's past, fungi bands, and group sings.

Quadrille dancers performed in Emancipation Garden. According to the local newspaper of the time:

*There were fancy dress balls at the Grand Hotel and
other hotels. And music was continuous. Tuesday
followed with a huge parade led by Moko Jumbi stilt
walker Magnus Ferrell. The parade included Zulus and
Indians, David and Goliath, bamboula dancers, bikes and
donkeys, Big Heads, Gypsies, and others. A horse
cavalcade followed at the end of the colorful parade of
floats, troupes, mummers, and orchestras.*

The rains were very strong during that Carnival, threatening to shut
down activities more than once; but there were no crimes or traffic
accidents, and there certainly were not any coup d'etats. In fact, peace and
harmony presided. And, as if to make peace, harmony, and indefatigability
symbolic of all Carnivals to come, the Duke of Iron calypsoed through the
streets of Charlotte Amalie singing a new song, "Rain Cyan't Stop De
Carnival!" Even now, that's still the watchword of every Thomian during
Carnival.

To top it all off, Carmen and Leo got married shortly afterward and, the
last he'd heard, they were still married. In less than twenty-four hours,
many of these very same groups would march in another Carnival parade . .
. possibly right into the biggest coup d'etat in the history of the Caribbean.

Voices. He continued to work his hands and wrists in a steady rhythm
twisting the tape more with each turn, stretching it. He could feel space
growing inside the tape's confines. Soon, the space would hopefully
expand to the point that he could achieve enough leverage to tear the tape or
to slip from its grasp.

He must hurry. Someone . . . those voices were coming through the
window.

CHAPTER 8
LEGISLATIVE CHARTREUSE

6:02 p.m.

As Al entered the Senate President's hideaway, flanked by Iree on his left and Lois on his right, the twenty-foot plexi-glass picture window that covered the majority of the south wall and looked out from the edge of the island of St. Thomas into the depths of the Charlotte Amalie harbor stared him in the face. The same engineer who designed Coral World Undersea Aquarium designed it. The presence of sea life and the sea itself constantly poured into one's consciousness. When covering the discussions on the fishing limits bill a year or so before, Al remembered hearing the French Town fishermen and the Senate leadership trade lampoons about the area being fished out or not. Al remembered seeing a few fast snapper, some slow grouper, and a parrot fish parade past the window as if to remind them all that they were being watched by a very interested constituency . . . or at least what was left of it! Another time when the Boat Vote lobby leaders were meeting with Teddy, Al was there to write a story on the "substantive discussions between the Senate President and the Boat Vote leadership about regulating the waste discharge by boaters into the harbor." Just about the time Teddy brought up the harbor pollution problem and the Boat Voters were trying to convince him that he was over-reacting, a huge clump of turds washed by the window which, of course, broke up the participants on both sides of the table.

The room spread out from this special access hallway which ran from the President's inner chambers at the Senate Office Building some twenty-two feet to the water's edge where the inner-sanctum was carved out of the volcanic rock and dirt of the island basin containing the most natural deep water port in the eastern Caribbean. It was equipped with everything one could ever need for long work sessions or meetings or for governing under siege. Two computers tied into the legislature main frame installed during Teddy's first term as Senate President. There was also a separate standalone unit with its own word processor where the President personally stored his own private materials. Only one other person knew the password sequences required to access that material if anything ever happened to

Theodore V. Morhead. That person was staring at the smallest octopus he'd ever seen. It had worked its way onto the bottom far end of the window and seemed to be observing them carefully.

The smallness of octopi still surprised Al, even after many encounters with them in the sea and having seen them in seaquariums and observatories such as Coral World located in a small community known as Smith Bay near the eastern end of St. Thomas. It was the only other place on these islands where you could see into the world of the sea like this. The old image of huge octopi must persist from his childhood experiences like *Twenty Thousand Leagues Under the Sea*. Al was beginning to feel as if he were caught in the grip of eight tentacles as it was. This little baby clinging to the window's edge was merely a reminder of his present plight.

As they emerged from the semi-light of the passageway, Al could see the black-and-white vinyl floor beneath him as if for the first time. The room was about twenty-five feet wide by forty feet long. The tiles were laid over a poured concrete floor in an alternating way so that the floor was checkered with black-and-white tiles like a huge chess board--which, like this evening, it often was.

"I and I do not'ing!" Rastafari leader Ras Ujamma I's bass voice ping-ponged off the window into the Caribbean and the black-and-white tile floor. "I and I don' be waitin' no more!" He reared up from the conference table in the center of the room, the casters on his chair screeching over the tile. "Where is Al Crist, me-sons?" He pointed the knurled index finger of his right hand at the men in their suits scrambling from their seats across the table from him and his legal counsel Attorney Edna Black. "No Rasta from des islands be t'reatenin' you, mon!" He was dressed in his usual flowing tropic-white robes "like dose worn by my people in Africa" he was prone to saying in about the same vein as former U.S. Senator Sam Ervin used to say that he was "just an ole country lawyer." Or, if the occasion seemed to require it, he would yell or shout or scream. Whatever was right for the impression he wanted to make at the time. Usually he foamed at the mouth just a little as well. Flecks of spittle clotted at the edges of his full flat lips giving him the appearance of being mad . . . an appearance he cultivated masterfully through careful planning. Otherwise his appearance approached that of the regal. He was a slim man, around six feet four inches tall. His body was strong and his muscle tone was excellent from his work at the West End Commune and the fact that he walked or ran everywhere he went on the island. When he wanted or needed to get somewhere fast, Ras Ujamma I didn't hail a cab--which was just as likely not to stop for him anyway since he was obviously not a tourist--no! He broke into a long-gaited gallop, his robes flowing and billowing behind him. His locks were matted together in clumps, further adding to his appearance of a mad man . . . locks of a priest to some. Ras Ujamma I's flat sloping forehead, long thin face with high cheekbones and squared jutting jaw seemed to have been chiseled out of alabaster.

He was "clear skinned." This meant that his skin was very light, similar to a "white" person's. Sometimes "whites" were also referred to as "clear skinned." As in most societies or regions where nearly everyone's skin coloration is similar, Caribbean peoples broke down their coloring by qualifying its degrees of intensity or tone. "Clear": light or nearly white. "Red": ruddy complexion with a reddish cast to it though these red people are usually moderately light-skinned. Red skinned people seem to come more from Anquilla than from any other Caribbean island. "Brown": Caramel or slightly darker. "Dark": Dark brown or nearly black in color. Finally, there was one classification that always amused him. That classification was "Dark, dark, dark". Islanders had a way of repeating things three times when they wanted to add special emphasis to what they said. "Dark, dark, dark": black skinned without the brownish tones. Ras Ujamma I, of course, rejected out-of-hand such attempts at classification of peoples of the Caribbean and on St. Thomas in particular by gradations of color. "Dat's de mon from Babylon talkin'," he would say. "No bahn here Virgin Islander gonna come up wid such as dis clear skin, red skin, dark skin shit! Only de white man, me-son--to keep us separate from each odder, to keep us in conflict as people . . . red against clear against Brown against Dark and Dark, Dark, Dark."

That pretty much described Ras Ujamma I's mood as he yanked Edna Black out of her chair by her left arm, turned his back on the suits and strode towards the passageway just as Al, Lois, and Iree emerged from its shadows.

"Sorry, I'm late." Al reached out his left arm, blocking the hallway as Ras I approached, Edna following close behind. "I was unavoidably detained. In fact, I'm damned lucky to be here or even be alive." He stared straight through Ras I's pupils into his brain, searching for the reasons . . . the answers. Like where is Frenchie? He felt his lips begin to tremble like when he was a child and was getting ready to cry. He tried to control himself. But, his mouth just wouldn't stop quivering. "But . . . but . . . you .

. . you . . . already know that, don't you, Ras Ujamma I?" Al dropped his arm and stomped off in the direction of the conference table in front of the wall that looked out into the sea. "I came here to talk. If you've still got the stomach for it, then let's do it!"

* * * * *

Al had interviewed Ras Ujamma I many times as well as other members of his movement, including the creeps that'd nabbed him and Frenchie. No sign of Frenchie according to Lois and Iree. Damn, he and two or three of those bastards had smoked ganja together with Ras I and others at the West End Commune. Even though Al was aware that he was taking a risk by doing so, he felt that, just like he'd done things in the Nam that he didn't really want to do such as eating dog in order to gain the confidence of the villagers, he now had to take such chances with Ras I and his followers in order to gain their confidence. Afterall there were those who tried continually to bust his chops for something . . . anything. The more vulnerable he made himself to being blasted the more likely that his enemies would find it out and use it against him. In fact, Ras I could use it against him right here and right now if he wanted to, if he really was the enemy, as the notes seemed to indicate.

For some reason, Al was confident that he would not say anything about the many times they had smoked ganja after working the Rasta's fields all day. They would discuss politics and economic philosophy, particularly the philosophy and politics of non-violent revolution, something which Al was somewhat of an expert at.

Ras I knew Al's background, his revolutionary journalistic roots. He had read Al's work on the counter-culture in the sixties and early seventies and on the Kent State massacre. He'd won a Pulitzer Prize for that one. He was a famous journalist. Ras I was sure he could use him.

Why the hell Ras I wanted him here was beyond Al's understanding at this point. Sure, they knew each other and Ras I was exploitive, but why could he possibly want to see me hurt or dead? Why try to force me to write supportive articles in light of the very supportive articles from the past. Seven articles on Rastafarian roots, music and culture wasn't enough to demonstrate that he clearly leaned in their direction . . . without a push!

He obviously was sympathetic to their attempts at getting the West End Commune off the ground, growing organic vegetables They were already feeding themselves and still had enough produce to go to the market and sell nearly every day. Despite his support, even participation in their activities, he maintained a professional journalistic perspective, which had earned him three Pulitzers and this job. His Rasta series was filled with subtle insights about the movement that only a participant *could* become aware of. Characteristic Al Crist.

As it turned out, the articles were quite well received locally and throughout the Caribbean. Even the major news sources which supported him in this job were sold on the idea of a series because as one editor put it, "the series contains a good deal of valuable material about the Caribbean as well as some solid insights into the region and its cultures." It also gave the Virgin Islands Rastas an incredible amount of exposure for their cause. All in all, Al had been a damned good friend to the Rastas and to VILA when it was officially chartered as the political arm of the West End Commune Rasta family. That was one of the main reasons he was here at this meeting in Teddy's "playroom". Not only did Esteban and Teddy want him in the meet because of their perception of his relationship with the Rastas but also Ras Ujamma I had demanded that he be present. In fact, according to Teddy, this Rasta leader had made Al's presence at the meet one of the pre-conditions to his own attendance. Al thought that to be a little strange in light of the VILA threat note, the attack on his boat and that little attempt yesterday morning.

"Rasta wan' know, what be dis Liberation Army t'ing, you talkin'? I and I don' know who dis does be, me-son . . . Rasta say dey t'ink you." He hesitated and with a sweep of his graceful slender fingers indicated everyone in the room except himself and Attorney Black, a maiden of some beauty and no little wit whom Al had discovered over the past couple of years. "All you! You make up dis Liberation Army t'ing to make Rasta look bad to de people."

Al had seated himself at the far end of the Virgin Islands mahogany conference table complete with a view of the water in the harbor and of the underbellies of the hundreds of sailboats anchored or moored there from all over the world. Ras I and Edna had followed him back to the table after a whispered conversation at the edge of the passageway. Iree and Lois had retreated back down the passageway to wait in the Senate President's office. He purposely scraped the malfunctioning casters on his chair loudly against the tile floor as he stood to go to the bottled water cooler in the furthest corner of the room from both the picture window (where the small octopus still stuck like crazy putty) and the conference table. He wanted the noise to do just what it did . . . disrupt Ras I's flow before that flow became an unstoppable flood. If that happened, they could never hope to stop him long enough to get any kind of agreement or understanding worked out . . . short of calling the police, that is!

Ras I's voice lodged in his throat like a sugar apple seed. His face flushed red. He turned toward the scraping noise and glared at Al with his gray eyes, a feature which added a strangeness to his physical appearance that approached fierceness and intimidated nearly everyone except Al Crist. Legal counsel also tried to stare him down with a slight smirk of disapproval on her dark pursed lips. She knew what he was up to.

Al smiled back at them as he left the table and shuffled to the cooler. Wonder if they still want to demand that I be in this meeting, he chuckled to himself. For some reason, he could only see the outline of legal counsel's full and gently sloping breasts as they pushed against her white silk blouse. It wasn't so much that Edna played to her sensuality with her dress as it was that if she tried to hide her sensuality she'd have to wear armor or something equivalent. Al remembered their lilac fragrance and soft smooth warmth many nights at the commune when they were the only two who could talk to each other about things other than revolutionary politics and agriculture the natural way. Her passion was boundless and bottomless.

About half way to the cooler Al realized that he probably needed the cold water poured between his legs to cool down the responses he was having toward Edna right here under the harbor in the midst of possibly the single worst crisis in the history of these islands.

"Attorney Black . . . please . . . show dese gentlemen." Ras I spit the word gentlemen as if he had just dislodged that sugar apple seed from his throat and was expelling it. "Show dese gentlemen our 'Haul Over Resolution'. Let dem see what VILA really stands for."

Edna Black fished a folder from her eel skin briefcase with her stunning caramel fingers. Her nails, perfectly manicured to about a half-inch long points, were copper as was the gloss covering her delicious lips. He remembered how they tasted all too well. "May I, Mr. President? Governor?" She paused to open the folder, glancing at Al as he ambled back to the table with eyes that were nearly copper themselves. "Mr. Crist?"

She was a stunning woman. Not just her fingers. Her entire being. She was the woman whom you pass on the street and stop suddenly in your tracks as if you'd just run into a wall. Edna Black was that kind of stunning. Being stunning helped her a lot too, no doubt about that.

Edna still felt a great passion for Al Crist. It had been a long time, three or four months now. Edna, too, remembered torrid nights huddled in a shack at the commune, their bodies glistening in oil lamplight as they made love in every conceivable position. Why he was now on the other side in this, she couldn't understand. She'd thought they had him convinced. That he understood. She'd at least thought that *she* had him. Edna stared at the open file in front of her.

As she bent over to read, the three gold threads dangling from her throat dipped deep into the darkness between her breasts . . . that lilac darkness that so intoxicated him. "Haul Over Resolution." She paused, sucked in a provocatively deep breath which swelled her nipples against the white silk of her blouse. "I'll only read salient portions, gentlemen. You can follow with your copies to make sure I'm not leaving out anything important."

Edna used space between statements well. Al remembered kidding her about being the Elvin Jones of legal pauses. She had giggled and then, without another word, had proceeded to screw his eyes out for the next seven hours.

Everyone nodded in agreement with her as she slipped copies of the agreement to each person around the table as if she were Madame Sosostris dealing out the Tarot cards. Teddy at the head of the table, his back to the octopus and the Plexiglas wall. Edna was to his right. Ras I was to Edna's right. They faced the wall window almost directly. (Al wondered if they had seen the octopus yet.). To Teddy's left was his administrative assistant, Hector Valdez. To Hector's left was Esteban and his executive assistant, Lydia Braithwaite. Al completed the rectangle.

"The Haul Over Resolution." Edna's luscious copper lips repeated.

"WE, the undersigned delegates to the United States Virgin Islands Conference of Rastafari duly elected in our separate districts of St. Croix, St. John, and St. Thomas to represent said districts at this Conference,

"NOW, hereby resolve:

"THAT this resolution shall be known as the Haul Over Resolution and shall be forever binding on its signators and on those whom they represent.

"THAT the organization be known as Virgin Islands Liberation Action (VILA).

"AND THAT the following shall be the governing doctrine to which all VILA members must subscribe:

"A.   There shall, in no circumstance, be any attempt by VILA or any group of VILA members, either formally or informally, to overthrow the duly elected governments of the United States Virgin Islands or the United States of America by force or violence;

"B.   In no circumstance shall violence or armed insurrection be tolerated by VILA, and any such attempts at any time shall be punished at the most severe levels by immediate banishment from VILA and from any other communal association with the United Rastafari Conference of the Virgin Islands.

"C.   There shall, however, be every legal and legislative effort and attempt possible made to change the structure of power in the duly elected Virgin Islands government in order to establish a more perfect order, one which in every way is in harmony with nature and which fulfills the basic needs of all Virgin Islands people."

"I submit to you, gentlemen, that these are not the words of assassins, terrorists or worse! In fact these particular words are the words of this man right here!" She nodded with a sly smile in Al's direction, drooped her slender face toward her chest as she finished and closed the folder in front of her.

"That's true, Ms. Black. I did help write the Haul Over Resolution. But that doesn't explain these, now does it, me-son?" Al skimmed three gray envelopes one after the other the length of the table to where she sat. Each one landed almost directly in front of her on top of the folder from which she had just been reading.

Startled by the sudden action, Edna opened the envelopes by reflex rather than thinking about it before she opened them. With astonishment she read the messages and passed them to Ras I. "Oh, I didn' know . . . ah.

Believe me, Mr. Crist . . . Al. Please." So that was why he was on the other side. At least now she understood. "I really didn't realize that you had been threatened, my brother."

Ras I turned his head away as if he didn't want to read the notes.

"Damnit, Ras I! Look there! Read for yourself." Al flung his arms out in front of him gesturing toward Ras I. In doing so he exposed the raw rings around his wrists from the bonds of his confinement in the Old Danish Warehouse. "Or look here at my wrists if you refuse to read the letters.

"Tell me VILA's not involved in this, me-son. Please." His lips quivered almost out of control. But he refused to let that happen. He struggled for control of every syllable as he spat out the words. "I mean, I have been kidnapped, beaten, and held captive by two of your top lieutenants and some of their men in cahoots with some Grenadians." Al almost broke down, then continued. "And they've still got Frenchie Bryan, goddamn you!"

Seemingly unruffled, Ras I stared at Al's eyes. Neither of them blinked. "How do you know dey be Ras I's men?"

Oh, Al almost smiled. Got his attention, did I? "I've sat around in your very own hut at the commune enough times and talked with you and your followers. Broken bread with them, worked the fields with them, wrote the resolution with them." He paused again to regain his failing composure, which was eroding as the beach does in the winter with the rougher seas. All he could conceive of in his mind was striking out at those who still held Frenchie. "I damn sure ought to know the bastards!"

Ras Ujamma I slammed the flat of his palm down on the Virgin Islands mahogany table. The letters and their envelopes scattered like Century plant seeds in the wind. The sound of Ras I's smack reverberated through the room just like a shot in a canyon or a cave. He turned his head away again, away from the conference table. Al couldn't be sure, but he would almost have sworn that there were tears in his gray eyes as he avoided Al's eyes.

"Gentlemen," he choked, this time without spitting the word. "If you would please excuse us. I and I not be prepared for dis turn of events."

Edna looked directly into Teddy Morhead's eyes and continued as if she were simply continuing the sentence that Ras I had stopped. "If it's okay, Mr. Crist and I will draft up an agreement of cooperation and support

tonight and have it finalized for your signatures by morning . . . early!"
Edna seemed to lift Ras I up off the tile floor chessboard as she guided him
forcefully toward the door. He seemed totally composed now. He'd only
lost it for a few short seconds. But he still allowed himself to be led away
by Edna like a pet.

"I can guarantee that our leader will agree to whatever we come up
with. He is truly wounded by this latest news." She paused, turning toward
Al. "My office at the house . . . in a half hour . . . okay?"

"Okay."

"Bring food and coffee . . . lots of coffee!"

"Okay."

"Gentlemen." She turned on her black spike heels and sashayed right
out of the room totally in control, as she usually was, with Ras Ujamma I in
tow as he seldom was.

Al sucked his teeth as he stood up. "Gentlemen." He too sashayed
from the room; the little glob of an octopus still ogled him from that
window into the sea.

* * * * *

It was nearly midnight.

"Look, let's hit it head on, Al. Otherwise we'll never get this shit done
by morning." She was trying--at least a little--to get down to the business at
hand.

Al was still trying to figure out why he *wasn't* at all trying to get down
to the business at hand. He knew the seriousness of the situation. But
somehow this woman, this luscious lawyer still had him spellbound.

"Okay, let's say, maybe, my client has a few--a mere handful, you
understand! --of extremists who have split from his influence. He can no
longer control them." She smiled, having decided something about
timesaving devices. She reached across from the chair where she was
curled up to a small lamp table with a single drawer in it. Opening the
drawer, Edna pulled out a mini tape recorder. "Okay?"

"Brilliant!"

Edna repeated what she had just said--exactly--for the tape recorder. Except that this time with every word she spoke she unbuttoned a button on her silk mahogany blouse.

"That could be understandable," Al responded. "Afterall, there are a lot of followers of the venerable Ras Ujamma I. It would be patently unfair to blame him or his movement for the unauthorized actions of a few renegades." In spite of himself and the circumstances, Al found himself touching her dark, almost violet nipples with his thoughts and his eyes as he spoke.

"There's more!"

"I certainly hope so," Al giggled. "Ah, I mean, I'm sure there is. I'm all eyes . . . I mean ears. I'm listening."

"Carefully, I hope!" Suddenly Edna covered her breasts by clutching her arms around herself. "Please."

"Okay."

"There are outsiders out there in the night somewhere right now with a bunch of renegades and maniacs who plan to overthrow this government, Al. They want a coup d'etat!"

"Is this revolution shit being greased as far as you know? By whom?"

"I don't know, for sure." Edna whispered despite the fact that they were all alone and she was supposed to speak to the tape recorder. Involuntarily she glanced around her to see whether or not she was being watched. Only Al was watching. She continued. "But I do know that both of the ones who approached us were Grenadians." She hesitated, as if just thinking of something.

"They said they wanted Ras I to join them and be their figurehead, their leader."

"But he refused?"

"Yes. Well, not in so many words. Not at the time. We told them that he'd think about it. But, really Al, he never had any intentions.

"And, they did say they were going to get *you* to write their story." She shrugged. "Hell, baby, that truly pissed me off, but I didn't take that shit seriously . . . not for a minute! Maybe I should've, huh?"

"How could you have known? But, hell, that explains the notes . . . the VILA connection."

"What do you mean?"

"They're trying to implicate VILA and Ras Ujamma I to the point where the only place they have left to go is to the bosom of the revolution . . . to them! Hopefully, by revolution day."

"Carnival Parade Day in this case?"

"You got it, sister."

"I know, brother. I know."

"All I know, Edna, is that people connected to your client are trying to kill me . . . and I'm the only person who's put together the V.P.'s secret plan to create a revolution here so the good old U.S. of A. can have an excuse to bring a military presence into the Caribbean. I just hope this document we're putting together will help, somehow, to stop all that."

"I just want you to show me, Al Crist. Show me where all the guns and assassination plots are hidden," Edna whispered in that throaty voice she seemed to naturally take on when she was not "on" professionally but was "on" in other ways.

Her voice was as smooth as the silk blouse she, once again, shrugged from her shoulders as she spoke, mahogany silk that slid down her ebony breasts as she breathed in slowly. The blouse material caught on her violet nipples for just a moment before slipping to the polished teak "decking" in the greatroom of her seaside condominium villa. It wasn't lavish or pretentious. It was comfortable and unique like she was, always full of little surprises and always stunning.

"Ras I says I'm to get you to listen, to believe that we aren't the ones doing this, no matter what those notes seem to indicate. And, I don't know how else I ever got you to pay attention to what I had to say, so." She licked her copper lips. "It's almost J'Ouvert. We could jump up just a little, that is if you still want me."

Al looked up at her ebony body, naked from the waist up, draped in a wraparound skirt from the waist down. He slouched comfortably in the pile of pillows Edna kept in the sunken portion of her greatroom instead of having a couch.

"I mean, you're not in love with that woman after just one night, me-son." The softness of her thighs teased his face, nearly touched his cheeks, his lips. "Are you?" The dark violet of Edna Black swarmed over him taking him into a spinning vortex of wild, delirious pleasure.

CHAPTER 9

J'OUVERT MORNING

5:30 a.m.

Tramp...tramp...tramp.
J'Ouvert mor-orn-ing.
Tramp...tramp...tramp.

The torches are all steady
in the darkness of the morning.
The youth are all ready
for the march into the dawning.
What are they tramping for?

Tramp...tramp...tramp.
J'Ouvert mor-orn-ing.
Tramp...tramp...tramp.

The obeah of love
fills the mountain streets
like jumbies from above
dancing without the least
idea of what they're tramping for.

Tramp...tramp...tramp.
J'Ouvert mor-orn-ing.
Tramp...tramp...tramp.

On your right side, a white man.
On your left, a red la-a-dy.
In front of you, a black man.
Behind you, a Tri-i-ni.
Oh, what are you tramping for?
Tramp...tramp...tramp.
We're all new born in our
tramp...tramp...tramp.

Tramp...tramp...tramp.
J'Ouvert mor-orn-ing.
Tramp...tramp...tramp.

Torchlight slipped in and out of the trees and buildings like campfires suspended in the darkness. Trumpets, trombones and steel pans calypsoed through the stillness. A faint smell of rum penetrated the collective breath of the revelers. The sweet aroma of burning ganja swirled through the Lignum Vitae trees that ringed the garden area . . . the trees of life. The lead band, Iree and the Gumbies, drew nearer to Emancipation Garden's parking lot.

It was J'Ouvert morning. The tramp was on.

Most trampers followed their favorite local band. However, some tramped behind the group that performed a particular calypso written specifically for St. Thomas Carnival because they believed it should win the title of Road March Song for that carnival season.

They shuffled slowly behind the band in a calypso, two-step rhythm with little or no additional movement from the waist up. The Tramp may best be understood by the non-West Indian as a calypso shuffle not unlike "the stroll" or the way Al remembered dancing to Maurice Williams and the Zodiacs' "Stay." He knew Jackson Brown had done a more recent version but that wasn't the memory lane version. In fact, Lois probably never even heard of the Maurice Williams version. He and Lois tramped behind Iree and the Gumbies. They were *the* youngest group in the J'Ouvert morning tramp this year, but due to Iree's great talent as a songwriter combined with Al's lyrical abilities, they were well on their way and were in the unusual position of having two songs being considered for this year's Road March honor which went traditionally to the song that was played the most during the carnival parades. Iree was very happy about his band's good fortune. He'd have been crazy not to be, but as he led them through the darkness of Emancipation Garden to Veteran's Drive along the waterfront, he was fearful, not elated. "It's a kind of fear I never experienced before," he had explained to Al and Lois earlier at the club between sets. Al had laughed, a lyrical but cynical laugh. "Oh hell, Iree, that's just the shakes, mon.

Everybody gets the shakes before a battle begins. 'It's traditional.'" he sang, mimicking as best he could an old island favorite.

.....Two . . . three. Two . . . three . . . and . . . one . . . two . . . three. Iree counted in his head as the Gumbies made the transition in complete silence from Al's favorite road march candidate to his own favorite.

> We gonna jump up and do it. Doit!
> Gonna jump up this year.
> We gonna jump up and do it. Doit!
> Cause Car-ni-val is here....

Iree Gumbs' raspy baritone voice lifted above the din of three trumpets, two trombones, a baritone horn and various drums as he belted out the chorus of what he felt was the Gumbies' best shot at Road March victory.

Al could see bands and trampers moving in from all directions now, converging on the Emancipation Garden and Veterans Drive area. The crunch was just beginning. Soon that one and only four-lane road on St. Thomas would be packed with early-morning revelers drinking rum, smoking ganja . . . many in costumes of one sort or another or more often than not parts of their own carnival costumes for the parades--a patchwork preview of Saturday morning's adult parade. They were all jumping up for J'Ouvert! Maybe, just maybe, this agreement he and Edna had finally drafted, despite heated interruptions, and presented to Teddy, Esteban and Ras I at four a.m. on J'Ouvert morning would help . . . maybe. At least Ras I's people would be trying to help flush out the real revolutionaries. He was pretty convinced now that the real VILA was not at fault. A sweet distinctive odor behind him took him back like a time warp to days in the Nam and later in the homes of hippie and yippie friends and political leaders as he covered the cultural revolution in the sixties and early seventies from the inside out. That was his style then. That was still his style. But Kent State did it to him.

He remembered that Doc Streeter had suggested that he be cool about smoking dope, and he'd agreed that was probably best. So, he now limited himself to smoking dope at sea or in some equally inaccessible place or at certain very special celebrations. J'Ouvert was usually one of those. But not this year. Not with lives and governments hanging in the balance.

104

* * * * *

"Screaming Monkey Art! Screaming Monkey Art! This is . . . ." Al hesitated. He knew he had to use his code, otherwise Santurce would never know he was the one out here in the middle of this shit. "This is Shakespeare in the Hamlets." Static hung like fog in the receiver. "Special Monkey needs assistance dumped about two-point-five clicks north of our last performance. Saturation requested commencing zero three hundred hours to zero three fifteen hours. Lower by point five clicks. Assist again from zero three twenty-five hours to zero three thirty-five hours. Do you copy?"

Through the heavy static, Al could hear a voice. "We copy you, Billy. Hold one for confirmation." The twenty or thirty static-filled seconds that passed while Al waited before he heard the click of the radio at the firebase seemed like several light years. "What's your theater, Billy? Over."

"The Globe. Over."

"Roger, Billy. Support mission acknowledged and confirmed. Time sync in five seconds on Mark. In five seconds the time will be eighteen hundred eighteen hours. Four . . . three . . . two . . . one. Mark!"

"Mark at eighteen eighteen hours. Over."

"Good luck, Billy. We copy your problem. Couldn't help hearing the director's feud with you before. A request from Billy in the Hamlets is a real special one to us here. We'll soften up the hearth for your homecoming just as much as we possibly can. You just tell us where along Stratford Von Avon we can make additional deliveries if needed. Over and out."

"Roger! And thanks Screaming Monkey Art. Thanks! Out." Al snapped off the radio. Might as well leave it here with Stinky. He and Poet certainly weren't going to need any radio where they were going now . . . into the midst of frigging hell. "Poet?"

"Yeah, Sarge. Over here with E.F."

"Looks like it's just me and you, Poet."

"What you mean, Sarge?" Poet looked up slowly from his task of carefully sealing off as much of E.F.'s ground up face, neck and chest as possible from the jungle air. He was already rotting in places.

105

"Captain Challenger has ordered us-- A1A--to hold our position at all costs."

"Jesus!"

"No. Challenger."

"Jesus! Us against a whole fucking company of NVA regulars?"

"I believe you have the picture firmly and precisely in focus, Poet; and they are my sentiments as well. So, I have already started in motion a little fucking ambush for the NVA."

"Guess I'd better finish up here with E.F. Too bad, you know, he's probably finished anyway since there's not gonna be no MEDEVAC chopper."

"What you got in that scheme-filled mind of yours, Sarge?" Poet sealed off the remainder of E.F.'s sausage chest with the last poncho he'd been able to scrounge.

"Like I said, Poet. A little fucking ambush."

"For a whole fucking company?

"Yeah, Poet." Al smirked. "For a whole fucking company."

* * * * *

6:13 a.m.

Car-ni-val all over de world,
that's what we be singing for.
Car-ni-val all of de ti-ime,
that's what we be wantin' for sure.
Durin' Car-ni-val all people be one.
Durin' Car-ni-val all we have fun.
Brothers and sisters under
the Car-ib-be-an sun.

We gonna jump up and do it. Doit!
We gonna jump up dis year.
We gonna jump up and do it. Doit!

Car-ni-val time is here!

Lois's lithe, muscular body swayed to the rhythm and to Iree's words. She was desperately trying to shut out everything but his words, the music, and the warmness of Al's hard body next to hers as they shuffled along in the glow of torches and the soft coming of dawn. Nothing could completely close off her mind from the fear. Not even her first experience with the greatest bacchanal in the Eastern Caribbean could overwhelm her with enough sensuality to blot out what was going down and without any of these thousands of people around her knowing anything about it. Those few moments with Al under the moon light on Bluebeard's Beach came to mind as she swayed along with the music, the steel pans pinging into the early-morning darkness as they stepped onto Veterans Drive heading west toward the Antilles Airboat dockage and strip.

That warm morning in the moonlight kept invading her thoughts, so she took Al's advice and tried to concentrate on it rather than avoid it. Almost like a sound track.

* * * * *

6:35 a.m.

The bastards couldn't fool old Frenchie Bryan. From the time those men had jumped him and Al on that deserted Peter Island beach, he'd known where he was. Their big mistake was in not doping him up or something. But he didn't fight or talk. He had remained docile and quiet so far. That way, they left him conscious. So he knew where he was right now, even after almost twenty-four hours of captivity. During that time they'd constantly moved from one place to another. But Frenchie had inherited an uncanny sense of direction from his father, a fishing boat captain originally from St. Barth's. Even blind-folded and disoriented as he was at first--being captured on a beach he wasn't familiar with on an island he didn't know very well--Frenchie Bryan knew that within a short time now the launch they were in would be pulling up alongside Remembrance. He couldn't, for the life of him, figure out why his captors would be taking him back to his boat, except . . . well, they did indicate often in their conversations that he wasn't to be really harmed. They also wanted to get through Drake's Channel and across Pilsbury Sound. No mean feat for a dinghy.

"Even if he be white," one would whisper, "he be a 'bahn heah' Virgin Islander." Others grunted agreement.

Frenchie's ears detected swells slapping beneath Remembrance just minutes before they arrived alongside the yacht.

"Shut ya engine, mon!"

"Okay. Okay."

The engine sputtered, stopped. Dead silence followed for a moment until their launch banged up against Remembrance's hull.

"Watch ya goddamned byoat, me-son!" Frenchie screamed, raising his voice for the first time since his capture. "Don't fuck me byoat's finish!"

"H . . . h . . . how'd . . ?" the one called Slider--who talked like he was the leader of this little band--stuttered.

Frenchie laughed. "Amazing, okay? Okay?"

"Okay. Okay," the leader called Slider mimicked. "Grab the Frenchman and put him aboard his master's lovely yacht . . . maybe he'll feel more at home," Slider's voice spit out at the four others still with him after all these moves in less than twenty-four hours.

A lot of manpower wasted to protect one prisoner and one boat, to Frenchie's way of thinking . . . unless of course they want to somehow try to use Remembrance's firepower rather than just keep it out of their way. They'd definitely need old Frenchie Bryan then. They'll be wanting Frenchie to show 'em how to use her weapons systems.

"The Frenchman'll get us across Pilsbury Sound in the yacht!" Slider hooted.

Hands clutched Frenchie's arms and legs. Fingers dug through his flesh to the bone. He felt himself lifted off his feet, hoisted high into the air and dumped like a sack of cassava on the well-oiled teak deck of his Remembrance. He could almost feel her shutter in disgust as the terrorists clamored aboard.

"Put the Frenchman below in one of the back cabins. Lock him in. You. Karim. You're a ferry pilot, right?"

"Yeah, mon," Karim chuckled. "I be dat, for sure, mon."

"Den, take dis byoat to St.Thomas, mon. In a hurry. De big boss wants to know how dis byoat's weapons systems work."

* * * * *

6:35 a.m.

Lois suddenly felt a fire far different from the fire of passion in her memories bombarding her body again and again with the new pressure of each karate star that struck her. The pain persisted and the penetration was somehow deeper than you might expect from the appearance of the wounds on the surface. It was almost mystical to her as she watched her nose break on the pavement in front of her and her face smash against the street. She'd seen Veterans Drive rushing up at her right through the still vivid memory of Al's crotch hunched against her lips until she didn't see anything at all ever again.

"Lois! Lois." He fell to his knees beside her work-of-art body crumpled now like a used envelope. "Oh, God. Lois!" He shook her once strong shoulders. Her mouth slacked open. There'd been nothing he could do about it. All anyone heard was a hiss and a quiet thud followed by two or three more hisses and thuds nearly simultaneously. All anyone saw was blood spurting from Lois's smooth caramel chest.

"Help! Somebody. Anybody!"

The crowd tramped past him and the fallen Lois without even knowing she was down or why.

"Plastic bag? Anybody?" Al begged as he worked on Lois's wounds just as Poet had on E.F.'s all those years ago on Monkey Mountain. Choppers hovered in his mind.

"Please. Someone. Any . . . medic! Medic!"

109

A few people stopped and made a large circle around them, trying to protect them from the trampers. Another person finally went off in search of the Emergency Rescue Squad and the police. Al felt like another person, himself. Old habits, bits of knowledge, fears crept into his mind as he worked. "Plastic bag? Anybody?" He yelled again while tearing his carnival t-shirt into strips. From a hand in the darkness of the circle of people around them came an A.H. Riise Liquors bag. Al immediately pressed the plastic bag against the gurgling chest wound just to the right of Lois's heart. Al remembered his Special Forces Drill Instructor at Fort Bragg telling them about sucking chest wounds.

"Make sure the seal's tight, idiots. Otherwise, the wounded man won't even breath long enough to find out how bad the wound really is." His unit was the first class of basic trainees at Fort Bragg, North Carolina since WWII. A great distinction, according to Drill Instructor York, to be trained by the Army's finest Green Berets and Airborne Rangers. Gung-ho!

Bit by bit it meant something, though, didn't it? You made it out of the Nam alive. Sergeant York was right about just about everything. Al realized that on Monkey Mountain where he had opportunity after opportunity to practice what York had preached.

Al kept pressure on the plastic seal as he gradually worked three t-shirt strips under Lois's limp body. Then he tied the strips in place very tightly to hold the seal snug against her sweet, bloody chest. He began to shake from the inside out. Hold on, mon. Hold your shit together! "Medic! Medic! Medic!"

The blades of a huey popped against the humid air above Monkey Mountain as Al squatted on Veterans Drive holding Lois's cold head in his lap, weeping.

* * * * *

7:25 a.m.

Ras Ujamma I had never before in his life felt indebted to a white man . . . and a continental at that! At the end of this J'Ouvert morning he certainly didn't think he liked that feeling too much either. Edna's assistant had brought him the agreement already signed by Esteban and Teddy. He signed it at three a.m. . . . something that he had vowed never to do . . . side with the established island leadership.

And, it was this feeling of indebtedness to Al Crist that was also forcing him to go against some of his other most basic beliefs in order to try and help him, now, when he badly needed help. Ras Ujamma I sucked in his pride and his beliefs with a deep breath. That was all part of owing. He knew. Ras I stuck out his thumb for the first time in his adult life.

A Rasta in a VW beetle with darkly tinted windows passed by, then slammed on brakes and backed up. The passenger door flung open seemingly by itself. "Come, mon. Come."

Ras I loped over to the VW, stooped over and tentatively coiled his lanky frame into the leatherette bucket seat amidst an atmosphere thick with ganja smoke and Bob Marley's "Redemption".

"Ras I, mon. A privilege, me-son." The driver grasped Ras I's hand in a handshake of the revolution. "I and I take you anywhere, mon."

"Tell me somet'ing, Wadabli?"

Wadabli put the VW in gear. "Okay, okay, me-son . . . but close de door." He smiled.

"You be one of de Governor's drivers, mon. You be a bass player in a reggae band, mon. You be a Calypsonian, mon. And, you be Rasta, too, mon."

"But I believe in cyars, mon." Wadabli laughed, pulling at one of his locks that fell down his back. "Not like you, me-son." Suddenly he looked at who was sitting next to him in his car as if, for the first time, actually realizing it was Ras Ujamma I . . . spiritual leader of all Rastafarians in the Virgin Islands. "Why you ridin' in a cyar, mon?"

"I and I must find de mariner Frenchie Bryan . . . and de byoat Remembrance . . . and fast!"

"Okay . . . okay, mon. Now please close de door, me-son."

Before Ras I was able to complete the act of slamming the door shut, Wadabli assisted him by pointing the VW toward Nazareth Bay on the east end of St. Thomas along the southern or Caribbean side of the island and gunning its engine.

"Dat's Al Crist's mate?"

111

"Wha'?" Ras I was recovering from the acceleration shock.

"Frenchie Bryan . . . de Frenchie dat owns de marina at East End Bay Resort?"

"Okay, me-son. He be de one."

"Dis got to do wit' de revolt?"

"Me-son?"

"Look, Ras I, I delivered de Governor a death t'reat message yesterday mornin' as I was instructed to do by dis renegade Rasta. He." Wadabli's voice broke. "He said he was speakin' for . . . for you, Ras Ujamma I . . . for you, mon!"

"No, mon. Not for Ras I . . . no me-son . . .! Never before. Not now. Not never! I and I never t'reaten people's lives . . . ne-ver me-son! I and I don' believe in killin'."

"Well, you may believe in somet'ing different before dis morning's over, Ras I me-son."

"Why you say, Wadabli?"

"Well, Al Crist told me dat dere be an assassination attempt on de Governor, de Senate President, and possibly others . . . dis mornin'! He believes a troupe in de parade will attack the reviewing stand. He sent me to get de Gyuard while he and Iree Gumbs prepare those in the reviewing stand to deal with an attack. I was on my way when I saw you, me-son wit' your t'umb waggin' in de air."

"My god! Al will be killed. Dey all be killed, if we don' get help in time. De islands will be devastated by dese terrorists. Cyan you not go a little faster, mon . . . a bit faster!"

Wadabli pressed the accelerator to the floor as they hit a stretch of crumbling concrete known as Donoe Road.

* * * * *

7:41 a.m.

Once he had purged the choppers from his mind, Al remained sure that he knew all anyone else knew . . . and a little more. He must've questioned everyone within a hundred feet or more of the assassination at least twice and the police also questioned every person on the list he had compiled. No one saw anything or heard anything except the hisses and thuds and the blood spurting from Lois's neck.

Only Al, who was actually next to her as she slumped to the pavement, saw the weapons that brought her down . . . three stainless steel karate stars with a red-and- black yin-yang symbol painted on one side. On the other side, VILA in blood red letters.

The police certainly puzzled over the jagged holes in Lois's neck and chest and abdomen. But Al didn't tell the police about the three karate stars. He hid them in his pockets. He also did not tell the police that the attempt had really been meant for him.

* * * * *

8:00 a.m.

"How'd you know to go looking for Frenchie Bryan?" Wadabli asked. "Al's woman came to me in a nightmare. I was at the commune trying to get a bit of rest, mon . . . and . . . she. It was just after we'd signed the "Agreement of Emergency Cooperation" which was drafted by Attorney Black and Al Crist."

"Wha? Come, mon?"

"I tellin' you, mon. De sister come to me!

"I be running t'rough a swamp of black arms clawing at me. I be moving sooo slow, mon.

"It be like runnin' in molasses. I be so scared dat I and I would pass out and fall into de morass . . . be swallowed up!

"At de last possible moment, when in my fitful sleep I and I be sure dat I and I be dyin' before I and I cyan wake up, dere she be, mon. Just dere,

113

mon. You know. She's not standin' or sittin' or floatin' . . . just really dere, mon.

"'Don' be afraid . . . Ras Ujamma I, most loyal servant of your people. I will let nothing happen to you this day . . . but you must get up now and find the mariner, Frenchie Bryan. Only he and Remembrance of Things Past can save us all this day . . .!'

"Den, she be as gone as she had been dere. I and I woke up in a sweat. Smoked some good meditation to understand and den began my journey . . . somehow knowin' I and I'd be findin' him or hoped."

"Hey, mon!"

"Yeah, me-son?"

"You mean dat's why I be takin' you to where I believe old Frenchie Bryan is being held?"

"Okay, mon. Yeah."

"Yeah, mon. Dat sister, she come to me too, mon. No shit, mon! She be telling me to drive towards Nazareth right away."

"Well, I and I be damned, mon."

As the VW careened around the potholes, sometimes as large as one of the miniature deer which scarcely populated the east end, Ras I gradually relaxed into the bucket seat enough to feel the ride. I'm beginning to understand, he thought, how people can get addicted to this riding stuff. It's easy on you and sooo fast.

CHAPTER 10

CARNIVAL COUP D'ETAT

8:20 a.m.

SHUF . . . FLE. SHUF . . . FLE. TRAMP. TRAMP. SHUF . . . FLE.
SHUF . . . FLE. TRAMP. TRAMP. SHUF . . . FLE. SHUF . . . FLE.
TRAMP. TRAMP.

Moving only to the rhythms of their own tramping feet, members of the
troupe listed on Les Trane's parade manifest as the "Oriental Carnival"
seemed to glide along Dronnigen's Gade. The street was barely two cars
wide to the narrow sidewalks. Shops selling Rolexes, Chanel,
Wedgewood, gold and black coral jewelry, t-shirts, post cards, and just
about anything else a tourist might be expected to buy crowded the
sidewalks on each side of what was commonly referred to as Main Street
just like the wild grasses and trees crowded against the pavement of the
island's roads. The shop doors were always open, releasing air-conditioned
comfort onto the sidewalks to entice potential customers who are hot and
sweaty in the Caribbean sun into their merchandise lairs.

SHUF . . . FLE. SHUF . . . FLE. TRAMP. TRAMP. SHUF . . . FLE.
SHUF . . . FLE. TRAMP. TRAMP. SHUF . . . FLE. SHUF . . . FLE.
TRAMP. TRAMP.

The trampers' bright saffron silk robes, the ochre sashes around their
waists with black patterns forming yin-yang signs all over the sashes and
their headbands matching the sashes, glistened in the Caribbean sun.

SHUF . . . FLE. SHUF . . . FLE. TRAMP. TRAMP. SHUF . . . FLE.
SHUF . . . FLE. TRAMP. TRAMP. SHUF . . . FLE. SHUF . . . FLE.
TRAMP. TRAMP.

The Oriental Carnival Troupe's huge float which followed the trampers
was built on an ancient U.S. Army deuce-and-a-half which must've come
over for military purposes at some point and remained on the island, much
like the tourists who come for a visit and never leave. The float was
decorated around the theme "Stars Before A Fall". It pictured a throne
toppling under the weight of huge karate stars falling from a
black-and-white sky. Each karate star showed a drawing of a particularly

115

important Virgin Islands "star" for freedom. Buddhoe. All done in saffron, ochre, and black. Queen Mary . . . Von Daneken.

The troupe from the beach at Peter Island. Same crepe paper. The same as what was in the Old Danish Warehouse, too. The parade, then, is going to be the battleground. Just like we suspected. Al couldn't get rid of the image of Lois's face drained of all its color and vibrancy there on the waterfront, smack in the middle of Veterans Drive. Veterans. Shit. That was a laugh. Even all his experience and training as a soldier and Vietnam veteran didn't help her, didn't keep her alive. He'd treated and sealed the wounds off perfectly, exactly like he'd been taught and had practiced in the jungles and rice paddies of Nam, but the wounds just seemed somehow to be too great, too deep. Those karate stars wounded far more deeply and severely than their surface wounds indicated. Lois.

SHUF . . . FLE. SHUF . . . FLE. TRAMP. TRAMP. SHUF . . . FLE. SHUF . . . FLE. TRAMP. TRAMP. SHUF . . . FLE. SHUF . . . FLE. TRAMP. TRAMP.

Al had sensed his balance going profoundly out of whack as if an opponent had caught him while he was double-balanced and swept him. But for that small yet meaningful slip, she would be here beside him. How much better would that be? They might all die here in this reviewing stand . . . today. After all, Santurce'd left them on their own. The first time in all those years either of them had ever left the other in the lurch like this when he needed help. When all was said and done, Juan did work for the administration. He had to keep that in mind. Juan's inability to act in this situation or to even give him any kind of information beyond the Macbeth allusion which seemed to indicate that he felt guilty about not being able to help was an overwhelming confirmation of his own VP conspiracy theory about this impending coup.

SHUF . . . FLE. SHUF . . . FLE. TRAMP. TRAMP. SHUF . . . FLE. SHUF . . . FLE. TRAMP. TRAMP. SHUF . . . FLE. SHUF . . . FLE. TRAMP. TRAMP.

Let them come. I want those bastards . . . and I want them bad! Al turned to his left. As he started to speak his voice caught in his throat as he realized that it was Edna Black, not Lois, at his side. "This is the Troupe. Be ready."

Edna nodded, turned to her left. "Be ready."

Iree nodded. To all those near him he shouted, "Spread de word, me-sons. Be ready."

"Be ready" spread like wildfire throughout the reviewing stands as the Troupe closed in on Post Office Square.

* * * * *

8:35 am

Behind Ras I and Wadabli lay the ruins of Bluebeard's Beach Hotel strewn across the sand among the coconut palms and seagrape trees. It was ruined by the last great upheaval in these islands . . . the Fountain Valley massacre on St. Croix. After those Rasta-looking types blew away all those folks at the Fountain Valley Golf Course Club House in 1973, there was a huge economic slump as tourism fell off abruptly. Bluebeard's Beach Hotel was a major casualty of that upheaval. In front of them, anchored about forty feet off the white sand beach, lay Remembrance of Things Past.

"I told you, Ras I, mon. I told you!" Wadabli pointed one of the slim fingers of his left hand he used to create the chords he played on his Fender electric bass toward the yacht. He almost doubled over with laughter.

Ras I slapped at Wadabli's head, grasping some of his thick locks. "Shhh! It not be over yet, Wadabli," he hissed into Wadabli's ear. He glanced around. "No gyuards, Wadabli. Strange, yes? No gyuards?"

Wadabli nodded. "How we get to Frenchie, me-son? I know." Wadabli struggled with more laughter. "I know he be on dat byoat, mon. I, Wadabli, know it."

"And, we have no byoat, Wadabli . . .?"

Wadabli controlled his laughter. "No. Den we be swimming out, mon?"

"Yes, mon. We be swimming out."

"Wadabli don' be swimming out, me-son . . .!"

"Mon!" Ras I sucked his teeth. "And you said you'd do anyt'ing for I and I."

117

"Anyt'ing else, me-son, but goin' in de sea? Dere's fish and shark and t'ing in dat sea, me-son." Wadabli suddenly realized he was talking to the space that Ras I once, but no longer, occupied. Only his white robe remained in a heap on the white sand.

Ras I knifed through the transparent blue Caribbean Sea, soundless like a green turtle, toward Remembrance. The sea refreshed his skin. As he swam, each stroke seemed to strengthen him. He knew he had a special purpose here that he had to dedicate his meditation to . . . entirely.

Remembrance was dark as he approached. No one seemed to be aboard as Ras I pulled himself up a rope ladder that dangled from the stern. Yet his deepest instincts told him not to simply believe what he saw. He sensed something . . . someone . . . on board.

* * * * *

8:37 am

Karate stars leapt from the fingers of the troupers.

"Now!" Iree Gumbs' voice carried like a bullet through the heat of that Friday morning.

As the troupers released their stars in some kind of choreographed unison, slivers of silver light spun toward the reviewing stands set up just below the bust of J. Antonio Jarvis. A wall of three-foot-square plywood shields shot up in front of the targeted area in the reviewing stands. The people all around the area dropped under their seats simultaneously, covering heads, eyes, necks with their arms and hands and their elbows. Just as they had been coached to do only a few short minutes ago.

As the sun glinted off the silver metal, Al thought for a brief moment that they looked like Congressional Medals of Honor hovering in the thick air the way they gleamed in the sunlight bombarding Post Office Square. There were tears in the eyes of many around him who had not been quick enough to get behind their chairs or the makeshift shields Iree and Al had helped people devise earlier. Many were being hit in the first wave. But Al knew, Iree knew, the governor and Teddy knew, the public knew they had to hold out through several waves of this attack until the Oriental Troupe no longer felt that it had a superior edge because of surprise. They all also

118

knew that as soon as possible they had to counter attack as best they could with themselves and the police, the National Guard Wadabli was hopefully bringing right now from the other end of the island, assembled civilians surrounding them now, anyone who could be enlisted to help. But, Al knew how hard it was for people not trained in the arts of combat to fight off professionally trained, seasoned insurgents.

* * * * *

8:39 am

Wadabli heard a crack from the decks of Remembrance and an echo across the glass-flat Caribbean sea. It sounded like a gunshot. He abandoned himself to the situation, leaving a slightly larger pile of clothing on the sand as he sprinted into the water, diving headlong into the clear cool sea.

Wadabli did not once consider the fact that he was one of the alarming number of islanders who did not know how to swim. He did not once think through what he would do when he got to the yacht . . . if he got to the yacht.

He did not know who shot whom or if anyone shot anyone. All he knew was that the leader of his Rastafari nation might be in real trouble--maybe even dead--and it was his, Wadabli's, fault.

The sea refreshed his skin and somehow seemed to guide his silent underwater strokes as if, by osmosis, Wadabli was learning to swim as he swam. A second shot erupted from what seemed to be below decks.

And a third, sending shocks through the calm sea.

For the first time since he entered the water, Wadabli became aware of the fact that he was really in the water. For the first time, he began to struggle against the sea rather than allowing it to continue to guide him.

For the first time water began to seep into his lungs.

Wadabli could almost reach out and touch Remembrance's keel. Just a few more strokes and he'd be there. He couldn't drown now.

He owed too much.

119

8:50 a.m.

There was something about this particular man in the heat of combat that made Edna Black's nipples swell and burn as she hugged against Al's back. They were "hunkered down", as Al put it, behind their shield. Edna was experiencing as much difficulty restraining herself from raping him right there with death in steel stars sailing through the air like virus spores as she was in understanding how she could be absolutely aching for Al to make love to her right after Lois's murder . . . and when she was scared to death . . . or at least scared as close to death as she ever had any desire to be.

For a moment, Al thought he saw Lois standing beside him. She glowed like white phosphorous. Blood dribbled from gashes in her chest and neck. The karate star that was heading directly for his unprotected right side sailed through her phosphorescence and, at the last second, veered away from him and into a wooden shield being manned in the VIP bleachers by the Governor's counsel and the Budget Director. It was like right out of Conan the Barbarian. Then she was gone.

Edna's throat quivered, spasmed as a barrage of stars hit their shield, forcing Al's body backwards against her burning breasts and aching loins.

* * * * *

8:55 a.m.

The best Frenchie could figure, there were at least two people still on this boat beside himself. The various creaks under foot were too close together in time and too far apart in distance to be made by the same feet. If he could only find a weapon before one of those sets of feet above him decided to explore below decks . . . to check on him. Of course, after that shot, he wasn't so sure there were still two of them.

Frenchie worked the end of the rope binding his hands to his feet through the last loop, allowing the rope to fall away from his hands as he pulled up. "Dey ain' no sailors," Frenchie snorted. "Couldn't tie a half-hitch if they worked at it."

Two more shots above decks cracked the dark silence. "Cheese n' bread!" Frenchie pulled the rope from around his ankles, muttering to himself. "Mus' be somet'ing to dis concentration shit Al is always talkin' 'bout, oderwise Frenchie still be tied up. Wha's dat Al calls it? Some Italian kinda name . . . kundalini or some kinda t'ing."

The deck above him suddenly groaned with a new weight. He knew it was different than what he'd been hearing because, in the hours he'd been alone below decks--probably near Bluebeard's Beach or Bolongo Bay--he'd become sensitized even to the lighting of a Pelican on the bow of Remembrance. This new weight on the boat came from the sea.

He scoured the below decks salon for a quiet weapon. Something. Anything at all. Nothing. The terrorists did a good job of taking everything that looked useable as a weapon out of the area. His own shackles would have to do. Otherwise . . . it was his hands. So be it.

Frenchie had overheard them talking about Remembrance. They couldn't figure out the weapons system, and he refused to help them. So, they decided just to leave the boat where it was anchored with its obstinent Frenchie first mate locked up below decks.

He knew he had to gain control of Remembrance and get her to the Coast Guard Dock on the Charlotte Amalie waterfront between the Legislature and "The Glass Bottom Boat" ticket booth. And it had to be fast! "Dem boys left a good t'irty minutes ago, he reasoned. So dey prob'ly attack already."

The sound of one of the sets of footsteps was unmistakable to him now. They were moving into the upper salon overhead. There had to be something the terrorists had overlooked. Frenchie just sensed something deep inside as he continued to rummage below decks for a quiet weapon. If only he could locate one of his spear guns.

* * * * *

9:15 a.m.

They escaped from the reviewing stands behind a shabby but still together chain of plywood shields just after that second withering barrage of karate stars. Their need, Al realized, was for larger support weapons and some kind of base of operations or command post and . . . reinforcements. There were just too few of them now. Wadabli hadn't returned with the Guard and just too damned many of the enemy. They had to close ranks and strike out in quick sorties. They had to take the enemy's initiative away . . . fast! As he led their regrouping, he guided them behind bursts of gun fire from the few police on duty in the area when hostilities ensued to the police station on Norre Gade. It was their logical line of defense and CP for now. It was the nearest brick or concrete structure . . . yellow nineteenth century brick. It will be a shame for those old walls to be chopped up by gunfire, Al mused.

"Iree!"

"Yo, Al?"

"Need you, mon!"

"Comin', mon! I and I be comin'!" Iree stumbled under the weight of a wounded child clutched in his trembling arms . . . his own left leg opened up to the bone along the calf line.

"God, me-son. Put down the child, mon!" Al scooped up the girl. "Hold to my shoulder." Al stood up, exposing himself to a new onslaught of stars. Edna leaped up and raised their shield enough to protect the four of them . . . just enough.

"We have to get all these people to the police station," Al muttered to Edna and Iree.

"I and I cyan make it on me own, mon. Don' worry 'bout de leg. I and I cyan take a bunch of people wid me."

"I'll take the little girl, Al," Edna gasped as she struggled with the shield.

* * * * *

10:10 a.m.

"There's just a few of us and a lot of them," Al emphasized as he, Police Chief Braitwaite, and Iree briefed the five men and three women who were acting as their squad leaders. "But I've got a plan."

122

The police station had been instantaneously transformed into a command post and a field medical facility of the most primitive fashion. Edna had left the little girl with a woman named Roebuck, an EMS who was heading up the emergency medical facility "Okay, mon. We could use one." Iree winced as Edna quick stitched and dressed his leg wound as best she could with needle and thread and lots of alcohol.

"After everyone gets to the station, we'll plan our counter attack. They may not anticipate that we would be so audacious as to go on the offensive. Somehow, we've got to get to Fort Christian, the legislature building, and the Coast Guard dock. The cutter's the only other major source of larger firepower nearby and the fort and the barn are the two major fortifications at this end of town. Plus, it gives us direct access to the sea." He shrugged his shoulders. "If we can pull it off."

Let's do it!" Iree turned his head away as Edna snipped the last stitch into place. "Wrap it to go, please, nurse." He tried to laugh. "I and I be in kinda a hurry."

Edna finished wrapping the stitched wound in strips of sheets confiscated from the jail laundry. "Be careful. These aren't like a doctor's stitches, Iree. They'll tear out easily. You need a lot of internal stitches on this one, me-son."

"A Rasta feels no pain." Iree tried to grin as he eased himself up off the stone floor, bracing his body with Mose's AK 47.

"That's good, Iree, because you're gonna have plenty reason to not feel it."

"Got any rounds left for that thing?" Al quipped.

Iree shook his head. "But it be an impressive walkin' stick."

* * * * *

There was an anti-war demonstration on the Ellipse the day Al Crist, Sergeant, U.S. Army and Whitman the Poet, AKA Paul Whitman, Corporal, U.S. Army were presented with Congressional Medals of Honor for "their combined actions during Operation Screaming Monkey far above and beyond the call of duty during which they continually risked their lives, engaging an overwhelmingly large enemy force by themselves, exposing themselves continually to hostile fire, which actions resulted in the elimination of an entire company of NVA crack ranger troops, and saved the life of a wounded comrade-in-arms." At first, the Army wanted to give the medal only to Al and present Whitman with a Silver Star. Al had said, to put it mildly, "no fucking way! Either we both get the medal or neither of us gets the medal, muthers!" They needed heroes and victories back in 1966.

"Hell no! We won't go! Hell no! We won't go! Hell no! We won't go! echoed over the expanse of the Ellipse, slithering through the marble sentinel city.

Al and Poet fluctuated between abject hysterics and festered ceremoniousness. They weren't sure whether they ought to hang around for their ceremony or run over to the Ellipse and tell all those chanting people to keep right on chanting . . . but add the names of their brothers and sisters who died in battles they really didn't want to fight. "All we are saying is give peace a chance." Then Al would lead the chant of the 57,000 plus names of the dead. What a powerful chant that would be.

They had some kind of power going for them that morning on Monkey Mountain too, Al remembered. At precisely two fifty-nine hours, Al and Poet had their M60 in place with a trip wire attached. Poet controlled it. He was to remain stationery and force the NVA back into the direction of the second fire mission when they fled in his direction after the zero three hundred hours artillery saturation.

Al humped his AK 47. He'd also found Promised Land's sawed-off shotgun near the same rubber tree on which he'd seen the headband impaled. Stinky's 16 was still working. Those two weapons were strapped to his back. His own .45 was strapped to his right hip. He was the hole-plugger. Any breaks in Poet's dyke . . . his field of fire . . . rigged up between his BAR and E.F.'s 60 and the edge of the mountain. Supposedly, nobody could get by him that way. If they did, however, it was up to Al. In essence, they were going to try and drive the NVA company down Monkey Mountain and mop up on them after two lethal artillery barrages when they tried to escape back up the mountain.

Screaming Monkey Art was good to its word. They dropped in better than twice the usual number of rounds during the normal 15-minute saturation mission. They hit so hard, and so few NVA came towards their crossfire ambush, that both Al and Poet wondered if they really needed the second mission. What the hell, they concluded. It's already been ordered.

As they moved to their second position, immediately south of the area just hit, Poet and Al encountered only two minimal threats--one half-dead NVA sergeant who tried to blow them all to hell and back with a grenade. He was like a living boobytrap. They just toppled him on top of his own grenade and dove away from him. The NVA sergeant was so weak he couldn't even crawl off of the grenade. So his body took the full impact of the explosion, saving their lives. The other encounter was a very live sniper. Poet spotted him when he was with his back to them. After alerting Al, Poet brought his BAR down on the sniper and let loose. The sniper never knew what hit him. Poet took his head right off his shoulders . . . in bursts of three.

Just as they got set in their new positions, the second barrage came in. It lasted only 10 minutes but was even more devastating than the first one. Out of the firey mess in front of them came two small assaults, both mounted by desperate men, many of them burning like torches in the early morning darkness as they charged. The guys at Arty had sent them some napalm rounds in too, right along with the regular rounds. Al and Poet mowed them down, the desperate human torches, as the torches ran at them shrieking. Al and Poet each had piles of burning bodies around them like campfires.

Then the helicopter came. Medics lifted Al, Poet, and Errol Flynn Brown into the clean quiet heavens. Poet was convinced they would, anytime now, see Promised Land strolling by. You see, Whitman the Poet was convinced that they were all dead, not just Promised Land . . . and possibly E.F. It was weeks before he finally realized that he and Al had actually pulled off that little ambush. When Poet came out of it, Al was sitting beside his bed as he had been doing for three weeks and four days. He sat and wrote sketches about their experiences in his unit and the guys he knew, both from the point of view as they all knew him in A1A and as a sleeper agent in a special intelligence network out of Plieku. His contact: Captain Juan Santurce, MACV, JAG (Judge Advocate General). One of the first to take a combined undergraduate degree and law degree, Santurce graduated and immediately entered the Army at the rank of Captain in its legal division, the Judge Advocate General. After a short time, Santurce was transferred TDY to G2 and assigned to head up a special intelligence-gathering operation in the central highlands. But he officially would keep his JAG address for cover purposes.

Al was a sleeper. To all that searched his military 201 personnel file, he would appear to be an 11B40--a grunt infantryman sergeant. Nowhere did his record show eight months of intensive counter espionage, anti-insurgency and Vietnamese language training at Fort Holabird, Maryland. "You may never be called upon, gentlemen, and if not, you must be content with your lot at the level you are assigned . . . infantryman, corpsman, medic, cook, whatever for the duration of your time in service. If you are activated, it will be with the special code that is included in your diploma package. That code on a plain blue index card is the only thing you could keep from the diploma package. Everything else that was possible proof of having been trained in deep cover intelligence operations was retained by the Army until discharge or declassification. Al's code name was Shakespeare. He presumed because of his literary background and degree. His activation code was HAMLET. He presumed once again due to the literary connections to the play. Or maybe because of the small Vietnamese towns called hamlets. Shakespeare in the hamlets rather than Shakespeare's Hamlet.

Al leaned his head forward as Lyndon Baines Johnson, President of the United States of America, stopped in front of him and placed the sky blue star speckled ribbon around his neck. For the first time since Monkey Mountain, Al trembled.

"Th . . . thank . . . thank you . . . ah, Mr. President."

"Oh, no." President Johnson shook his head.

"All we are saying . . . is give peace a chance," the crowd on the Ellipse was still chanting. Still no one chanting the names of the dead.

"No, son . . . Sergeant Crist. Thank you!" It almost looked like the Old Man had tears in his eyes as he snapped a salute to Al and turned crisply on his heel.

* * * * *

10:21 a.m.

Rifles cracked nearby. Machine gun fire strafed the entrance to the old police station on Norre Gade. Chunks of faded yellow stone flew through the air, smashing barred windows at the entrance to the station where several police officers stood guard.

"Look, me-son, I and I know it be cra-zy." Iree shook his locks back and forth, slapping them against his shoulders trying to get rid of the dust as he huddled behind a turned-over Sergeant's desk with Edna and Al. Yellow particles showered into the air around him like an aura. "I and I know dat, mon. But, I and I be seein' what I and I be seein'." Tears welled in his dark, pain-pinched eyes. "It be me brudder, me-son. He be wit' I and I durin' de skirmish, tellin' I and I what to do, how to act.

"Hallucinations under stress--particularly the stress of intense combat--are certainly a matter of record, Iree."

"Yes, mon. Yes. But, even if dat be true, it be also a sign dat me brudder still be alive out der . . . out der . . . somewhere.

"He be so real, me-son, dat I and I could reach out and touch him . . . and did on several occasions. Yes, mon, I and I could actually feel him, like a solid, material person . . . like I and I or you.

"And he be sayin', 'hang in der, Bro. Stick it out wit' Al, me-son . . . help be comin'. Relief be on de way, Bro!'

"His voice sounded real as his flesh felt, so I and I stuck it out while you all retreated."

"You know, Iree . . . Al? I had my own personal combat hallucination as well." Edna eased herself up from the floor now littered with glass shards and chunks of the police station. "I saw a karate star heading straight for Al's right side. Then it veered off into the wooden shield next to us for no apparent or visible reason. That was almost a ninety degree angle!" She turned towards Al who stood beside her, leaning on a carbine, and gawking at her as if he'd seen a ghost. "I saw it coming, but I couldn't warn you in time, baby." She brushed his cheek with the fingertips of her left hand. His flesh was afire. "If the deflection had not taken place when it did, you'd be dead now." She stopped herself before she said aloud what she was thinking as the rest of her sentence. 'Instead of providing me with a

127

continuing focal point for all my passions and wildest sexual fantasies.' He would be even more in need of her now, she knew, because of the ungodly murder of Lois. If she could only help ease his pain. Oh, yes.

Al pulled back from her touch, from the still lingering scent of lilacs that seemed to cling to Edna despite the stench of gunpowder and blood, which was threatening to absorb them all. He didn't mean to shrink from her. "I'm sorry. I didn't mean." He appreciated what she was saying, doing. But it was automatic . . . reflex . . . probably it was the combat mode he was in. "I never saw it." He shrugged, tried to smile at her, touched her hands. "Too busy keeping alive, I guess."

"Well," Iree hocked. "I and I be needin' a rifle dat der be bullets for." He leaned on his brother's AK-47.

"Get a carbine out of the arms room in the back. Better make sure everybody that can shoot is armed. I know they should be by now. The cops are taking care of it back there. But, I want to be absolutely sure that we have every man and woman who can shoot a weapon to be armed. This counter-attack of ours is going to require all the fire power we can muster."

"Okay, me-son. Come, Edna. You cyan help."

"Okay, Iree." She moved off towards the rear of the building, following in Iree's footsteps.

"When we start," Al yelled after them, "first priority is gonna be making sure that Esteban and Teddy get safely to Teddy's underground hideaway under the Senate building. Once we get them in there and seal it off, nobody can get at them."

"Yes . . . me-son. Give a yell when you be ready."

"I'm going to get them out of the cell block now. We've got to be moving in an hour."

Machine gun fire spattered the building again. The police guards, Al, and dozens of citizen soldiers, now armed to take back their downtown, slouched towards the back of the room, away from the windows. Iree and Edna ducked into the hallway leading to the arms room.

"Sooner . . . if possible." Al chuckled almost inspite of himself. "Much sooner."

10:47 a.m.

"I know you've never done this shit before, me-son, but you've got the genes for it. I just know it!" Affecting the island mode of speech to emphasize the personal nature of what he was saying, Al continued. "But, mon, you be Promised Land Gumbs's bruddah."

"Well, me-son, at least Chief Braitwaite be a vet."

"All my experience screams at me that these terrorists were not prepared for any real resistance. That's why they're trying to keep us pinned down in here."

"Maybe, retreatin' to dis place not be such a good idea?"

"Maybe not, Iree. Maybe not."

"But you cyan get out t'rough de tunnel, me-son."

"T'rough what tunnel, Chief?"

"Der be a big, big tunnel dat run from under de arms room all de way into de fort basement."

"That's it!"

"What's it?"

"Instead of trying to reach the fort and the Coast Guard dock by taking the parking lot area which is what they might expect us to do, we'll pull a little surprise of our own.

"Chief?

"Yes . . . mon?"

"Put your best combat man in charge of your police forces. They'll remain here.

"We all go through the tunnel into the fort. Iree, you and Chief Braitwaite split up our troops.

"Chief. You take your troops out the back of the fort and establish a cordon line between there and here. Once that's set up, the police reserves you held back here can get out and sweep back up Norre Gade with your cover."

"Okay."

"Iree? You take your group out the front of the fort and cut off any access to the Legislature and Coast Guard dock."

"Okay."

"Listen, me-son. This will be the toughest fight, believe me. Until Chief and the police reserves sweep up behind them, you'll be on your own. So, be real careful, okay?"

"Okay."

"When you achieve the dock, secure the cutter right away, me-son. There's at least two machine guns mounted on her and no telling what else is in the boat's weapons cache."

"Yes, mon!" Iree grinned. "Yes."

"I'll take Edna with me. We'll get Esteban and Teddy locked safely away in the bowels of the Senate building and then come out to help you, Iree." He slapped the young man on the left shoulder. "Hopefully, you won't have to hold out up there all by your lonesome for long."

* * * * *

10:50 a.m.

"Move it, mon. Move it!" Al practically pulled Esteban and Teddy into the cavernous passageway carved out of the rock of the island. Chief Braitwaite's and Iree's groups of rag-tag citizen soldiers shuffled ahead of them armed with shotguns and carbines that hadn't been cleaned in years it seemed, handguns and semi-automatic rifles captured from criminals, machetes, and anything else they'd been able to get their hands on as if they were on a road march. Their flashlights and lanterns bounced among them in the blackness of the cave-like passage.

Edna, following Teddy and Esteban, dropped down through the trap door in the arms room. "Close it down," she yelled at the silhouette leaning over the lighted rectangle above her. The trap door clunked into place. It

130

was dark above her now as it was ahead of them except for the bouncing lights of the people. As she turned to face the dark passageway, she flicked the switch on the large spotlight-type battery-operated lantern hitched to the ammo belt cinched loosely around her waist. Its beam spread like butter over the entire passageway in front of them.

"Okay. Let's move."

"Okay, Al," Teddy slapped him on the ass. "It's fast break time."

"Okay . . ." Esteban muttered. "Okay. Let's get it over with."

The musty passage reeked of something akin to brimstone. The walls sweated seawater in oily droplets, iridescent in the cream yellow beam of Edna's lantern as they followed their two platoons of citizens towards the basement of Fort Christian.

* * * * *

11:11 a.m.

"My God."

Behind one of the scrolled pea green columns framing the legislature's main entrance, Al clutched Edna's face to his chest, holding her eyes away from the streets with his arms as he ground his fists into his own sockets.

Was he seeing things?

The bodies of Virgin Islanders, who less than three hours ago had been spectators at the Carnival parade were strewn over Veterans Drive and Emancipation Park like flamboyant leaves covered the goat cluttered road through Smith Bay in the spring. Al peeked around the pillars again. The bodies were still there, mostly beyond the black wrought iron entrance gate to the circular gravel driveway in front of the chartreuse building which housed the Virgin Islands Senate.

As Al looked out over the slaughter, he remembered the three basics of combat. Enemy. Weather. Terrain.

The enemy faced them across Veterans Drive. They were trained professional revolutionaries. They were well equipped and supported by APC's. They outnumbered the locals two or three to one.

The weather was clear and hot. Except for the bodies and the gun fire, to look upon what was left of this morning was to look upon just one of the hundreds of perfect Caribbean mornings when the sky is nearly cloudless and the sun is caressingly hot, the sea is flat and clear as glass, the breezes off the Sahara rattle palm fronds and cool the sun soaked air, and you feel as if everything is transparent . . . like a meditative state.

Finally, he scanned the terrain. The driveway sparkled white in the near midday sun. Inside the circle of gravel was grassy with hyacinths scattered around a granite fountain in the center. Beyond the driveway as it left the complex was a continuation of the wrought iron fence for a few yards to the end of the property. Along the property line between the Virgin Islands government and the United States government's Coast Guard facility, the legislature's fence separated them with stone on the bottom and wrought iron embedded on top of the laid stone all the way to the harbor edge.

Between the fountain and that part of the fence stood several large trees. The kapok tree, with its spreading branches and roots dangling from them to the ground, provided the best cover, and it was the closest to the fountain. And, Al thought he saw a hole blown in that far wall just above the dock area. The flamboyants on either side of the giant tree provided some shadow but no cover. Their limbs were too high off the ground.

He and Edna had successfully stashed Teddy and Esteban in Teddy's sanctuary. They'd established communications with the outside world using COMNET, a special communications system established by the consortium Al worked for. Finally, they sealed the two leaders off from the same outside world and closed off all entrances as they left to help Iree and the Chief.

Al spotted Iree, hunkered down behind what was left of the pilings along the Coast Guard dock. Sporadic but heavy gunfire kept him and what was left of his platoon pinned with their backs to the harbor.

Chief Braitwaite and his platoon were getting the shit kicked out of them on the far side of Fort Christian from the best Al could tell. But, somehow, they still seemed to be holding. In fact, the Chief and his people were all that was left between them and being pushed right into the same Charlotte Amalie harbor he'd been looking into from Teddy's hideaway only minutes before. In the distance, the rumbling of APC's seemed to portend their ultimate doom.

132

Edna wiggled from the grasp of his arms just enough to look upon the field of battle for herself. "Sweet Jesus," She turned her head away from the battlefield and back into the stench of Al's shoulder. "Sweet Jesus . . .!"

"Looks like Iree's pinned down over by the dock. Got to get to him . . . somehow." He caressed her hair, still faintly scented . . . with lilac. "You stay here . . . guard this entrance with your life."

She sobbed into his chest in response.

"I mean it, Edna!" He pulled her face up towards his. "With your life!"

The kapok tree's dangling roots would be the first cover point to go for. Then hug the shadows of the flamboyants to get to Iree.

She nodded, tears still rolling down her cheeks but, now, silently.

"Do you understand me?"

She nodded again as she locked and loaded her carbine. "Yes. I un-der-stand."

He kissed her forehead and her cheeks wet and salty with tears. "It'll be okay, Edna. I promise."

Then, like a ninja, his chest no longer touched her shoulder. He was already out of sight behind the granite fountain dominating the center of the circular driveway as the first APC appeared at the top of Mafolie hill, but Edna's lilac still clung to his stinking clothes.

* * * * *

11:20 a.m.

Al stumbled, completely winded and head thundering with adrenaline and exertion, into the makeshift command post bunker just in front of the Coast Guard Dock. Iree and three of what was left of his platoon slouched behind broken and burned pilings they had been able to stack in front of the dock. He was attempting to re-wrap his leg with strips of his own shirt for the second time in the last hour since Edna's stitches ruptured through his flesh and dangled uselessly from the bleeding lips of his now open wound.

"'Course, de first t'ing de bastards be doin' is sinkin' de Coast

Gyuard cyutter." He shrugged in greeting. "So we don' even have no machine gun."

"So that's how you got pinned down here, me-son?"

"Yes, mon. Yes."

"Shit. We need a break, here. Where's that damned Wadabli and the good old NG cavalry when you really need them?" Al clenched his jaw so hard that he thought he might break his teeth. "Goddamnit!" He reached for the bandages as Iree continued to fumble with them. "Here, let me wrap that, me-son. I can get more pressure on the bandage in the right places. I've also patched up a lot more wounds than you."

"T'anks, mon." Iree gave up the bandages to Al. "Have pa-tience, me-son. Have patience. Dey be here, pret-ty soon." He smothered a chuckle. "In Virgin Islands' time."

"That's what I'm afraid of, me-son," he snorted. Al checked his ammo pouch. "Hey, mon. You know the Virgin Islands' saying, 'You got to take the lime with the sugar?' Well, I've got some ammo, but I only have three clips left."

Iree winced as Al tied off the bandage as tightly as he could without cutting off the circulation. "And dat's de sugar of it, mon?"

"That should put enough pressure on the wound to keep the bleeding down for a much longer time." He tried to look confident, ignoring Iree's question. "It's only oozing, not really bleeding too bad. So, hopefully, the thick layer of rags I applied to the wound will keep the bleeding in check until we can, somehow, get you to a doctor.

"Me-son, you jus' don' know de whole lime of it. I almost got to laugh, you know."

"About what, me-son?"

"The *only* ammo we got left be yours!"

* * * * *

Noon

The sound of what seemed to be locomotives filled his ears even though he knew there were no trains on St. Thomas. Yet, Alfred Crist knew that sound! It was distinct from the whistling of the rounds being lobbed at them by the four APC's that were now seemingly set in their positions, content to lob occasional rounds from Mafolie Hill where Iree's wreck of a jeep still sat, past the garden onto Veterans Drive. Most of them so far had exploded harmlessly in Charlotte Amalie harbor behind and to their left as they faced the insurgents.

Al felt blood rush to his face. His head pounded as he suddenly began to laugh, almost uncontrollably. He deduced easily that since there were no railroads in St. Thomas the only thing that could possibly sound like a locomotive in the air had to be rockets. "It's Remembrance, goddamnit!" He hugged Iree pounding him on the back with his fists.

Another rocket roared overhead like an air born locomotive, exploding almost immediately after the first one in the Emancipation Garden parking lot where the insurgents had set up their front line. The rockets shattered vehicles in every direction, burying chunks of sheet metal and steel deep in the pocked and cracked asphalt-patched concrete.

Screams of the wounded and burning enemy filled the noon hour air. Suddenly the seemingly fixed APC's began to move quickly to flank the garden area. Shells whistled from their long barrels sending huge vortexes of the Caribbean Sea spewing into the air.

"They've got to try and take us before Remembrance lands."

"Yes, mon. And, we gotta stop dem!"

"I-ree! I-ree! Look, der, mon!" One of the nameless citizen soldiers in Iree's platoon pointed in the direction of French Town.

Iree and Al shaded their eyes from the sun staring in the direction the young man pointed. There, bobbing around on the sun-splashed harbor was a flotilla of fishing boats, some with masts and oars, some with outboard or inboard engines. When the shelling and firing diminished, they could hear cheers and screams bouncing across the gleaming water.

"Cheese 'n bread, me-son. I and I swear to the almighty Ja dat be Frenchie in de lead byoat."

* * * * *

"If you don' be wit' we, den you be against we! You do no'ting more for nobody else, mon! Ever!" Slider's thick mouth muttered, curling like a tell tail in the wind as he slid from position to position stalking Al. "Fist and me will see to dat."

"Coup de uber alles!" followed closely behind Slider as only a Fist could.

"Get across the fort parking lot and come in behind that bunker, Fist. I'll come right at 'em and draw deir attention. Den you hit Crist. Quick. Now, move out!"

* * * * *

As Ras Ujamma I leaped to the task of securing Remembrance to the dock, Al spotted Slider closing in on the bunker. Shit, they were down to the one clip of ammo in his AK after he held off that last assault. He only hoped the enemy didn't know that.

A great cheer swelled from the citizens-turned-soldiers. Al caught Remembrance out of the corner of his eye before he swung his view back to the conflict in front of the Coast Guard dock. Remembrance slid easily, perfectly up beside the dock. The shock of the rockets to the enemy forces had been so great that action was down to a spray of fire, a momentary isolated firefight, here and there. The cheers from his troops grew louder as the first French Town fishing boat docked behind Remembrance. Twenty Frenchie fishermen jumped off the boat armed with grappling hooks, spear guns, flare guns, pistols, shotguns, scaling knives . . . bandanas wrapped over their heads so they looked like Bluebeard's crew come back to life. Al didn't spot Frenchie on the boat even though that was the one Iree thought he had seen him on.

Suddenly, Slider charged headlong at the bunker. "Death to Al Crist . . . traitor! Death to Al Crist . . . traitor!" As he ran at them, he fired bursts of three at the bunker, pinning Iree and his cadre down as well as Al.

136

Al just couldn't figure out why this idiot, whoever he was, was charging right at him like this. He was just asking to die. There was a break in the firing. Al slid his head out far enough to see that Slider's weapon had jammed. Al fired. Slider went down, yet he began firing at Al again as he lay squirming on the street. Al fired again and again until Slider no longer was able to slide or pull the trigger.

"Al, behind you!"

Al whirled and fired at Fist charging at them from the rear. Nothing happened. He was pulling the trigger on an empty clip.

"Al! Catch!"

Al glanced towards the voice of Ras Ujamma I on board Remembrance and spotted a spear gun sailing through the air towards him. He dropped his AK and snatched the spear gun, as it seemed to float into his waiting hands.

Fist seemed frozen by surprise or something for a few seconds. Suddenly, Al realized what was going on. This guy figured he was safe. Al's weapon was empty. All he had was a spear gun, and this guy figured this to be a regular spear gun with a line attached to the spear which would limit its range, not a specially-designed Frenchie Bryan gun.

Okay, Al almost chuckled to himself. He aimed as Fist seemed to finally make up his mind to shoot and pulled the trigger releasing the spear. It hit Fist directly in the heart. As he pitched backward, his finger froze around the trigger, firing round after round into the ground and then into the clear Caribbean air until there were no more rounds to fire and no one left to fire them.

Al leaped towards Remembrance. Ras I was completing the loop in the last rope as Al approached, his right hand outstretched, his left hand grasping Frenchie Bryan's specially designed spear gun. "Ras I . . . me-son . . . I am in your debt. I am truly in your debt."

Ras I finished off the slipknot and embraced Al as he approached. "No, me brudder. Now, after all you been t'rough, I and I only hope we can be even."

As they released their embrace, Al responded, "If that is what you wish, me-son, then that's how it will be. You can count on it!"

"T'ank you, mon. T'ank you, bruddah." Ras I paused, as if to draw on some special inner strength. "Keep well."

"I will. And you, too, Ras Ujamma I. Now, it's time for you to lead the mop up operation."

"Yes, mon." He grinned. "Yes."

"Good luck, Ras I . . . and, thank you, mon . . . thank you."

"No problem. T'ank you, mon."

"You see Frenchie Bryan anywhere? Is he okay, mon?"

"Yes, mon. Yes. He be wit' de Frenchie's byoats. Frenchie be comin', mon. Frenchie be comin'."

Ras I waved, as he seemed to glide toward the end of the dock nearest the Legislature where boat after skiff after raft after yacht cruised in and dropped off loads of armed citizens. Ras I's Virgin Islands Volunteers. He could hear, now, the rumbling of large trucks and jeeps along Veterans Highway behind them. The National Guard.

"Here comes the cavalry behind Wadabli's VW!" Iree screamed. "I and I be tellin' you, me-son. Dey be here in Virgin Islands' time."

"You did, me-son. You sure did tell me!" Al thought he caught a glimpse of his first mate on the fly bridge, probably looking for one of his spear guns.

"Frenchie! Frenchie!"

"Yo, Cap'n!" Al heard from not too far behind him.

"Frenchie?"

"Up here, Cap'n!" Frenchie Bryan waved from the fly bridge ladder. "Come aboard."

"Frenchie . . .!" Al leaped aboard Remembrance and made for the fly bridge.

CHAPTER 11

LORD WADABLI

CALYPSO KING OF THE WORLD

The packed stadium pulsed with Calypso music as Al and Edna slipped and slid their way through the thick crowd from the pate stand to the south gate where they were to meet Teddy. The Calypso King of the World finals had to be postponed due to concerns about the coup attempt, but there seemed to be more people trying to get in this year than ever before.

The final calypsonian, Wadabli, took the stage amidst flashes and sounds like gunfire. "He and Iree put this number together in less than twenty-four hours. Unbelievable!" Al rolled his head from side to side in rhythm with the music.

We goin' jump up,
jump up all night.
We goin' jump up
and jam, jump up and jam.

No down-island rude
boys and no vice president
goin' take away
our gov-ern-ment . . .
de free-dom we've sowed
with the blood we spent.

We goin' jump up,
jump up all night.
We goin' jump up
and jam, jump up and jam.

No matter how dey
try to invade us,
all o' we goin'
pro-vide re-sis-tance.
All o' we goin' say

you cyan't defeat us!

We goin' jump up,
jump up all night.
We goin' jump up
and jam, jump up and jam.

As he exited to fireworks and the heavy particulate fireworks fog drifting downward onto the stadium seats, Ras I seemed to materialize in the mist, a telegram in his hand extended toward Al who pulled the telegram from his new friend's callused fingers, ripped the end off the envelope, and opened the folded yellow page.

CONGRATULATIONS, SHAKESPEARE. ANOTHER HIT.

J S

To contact Timothy Brannan or order additional copies of *Adventures in Another Paradise* or copies of his other works: *Into the Elephant Grass: A Viet-Nam Fable*, *TEACH*, *Manhattan Spiritual*, and *'74: A Basketball Story*

please shop, write, or e-mail as follows:

www.amazon.com

Gemini Publishing
2828 N. Atlantic Avenue, Apt. 502
Daytona Beach, Florida 32118
[multiple copy discounts available]

tbrannan@cfl.rr.com

www.ingramcontent.com/pod-product-compliance
Lightning Source LLC
Chambersburg PA
CBHW060231180626
46813CB00007B/3041